My
Almost
Epic
Summer

adele griffin

speak

An Imprint of Penguin Group (USA) Inc.

For Erich

SPEAK
Published by the Penguin Group
Penguin Group (USA) Inc.,
345 Hudson Street, New York, New York 10014, U.S.A.
Penguin Group (Canada), 90 Eglinton Avenue East, Suite 700, Toronto, Ontario,
Canada M4P 2Y3 (a division of Pearson Penguin Canada Inc.)
Penguin Books Ltd, 80 Strand, London WC2R 0RL, England
Penguin Ireland, 25 St Stephen's Green, Dublin 2, Ireland (a division of Penguin Books Ltd)
Penguin Group (Australja), 250 Camberwell Road, Camberwell, Victoria 3124, Australia
(a division of Pearson Australia Group Pty Ltd)
Penguin Books India Pvt Ltd, 11 Community Centre, Panchsheel Park,
New Delhi - 110 017, India
Penguin Group (NZ), 67 Apollo Drive, Mairangi Bay, Auckland 1311, New Zealand
(a division of Pearson New Zealand Ltd)
Penguin Books (South Africa) (Pty) Ltd, 24 Sturdee Avenue,
Rosebank, Johannesburg 2196, South Africa

Registered Offices: Penguin Books Ltd, 80 Strand, London WC2R 0RL, England

First published in the United States of America by G. P. Putnam's Sons,
a division of Penguin Young Readers Group, 2006
Published by Speak, an imprint of Penguin Group (USA) Inc., 2007

1 3 5 7 9 10 8 6 4 2

THE LIBRARY OF CONGRESS HAS CATALOGED THE G. P. PUTNAM'S SONS EDITION AS FOLLOWS:
Griffin, Adele. My almost epic summer / Adele Griffin.
p. cm.
Summary: Stuck babysitting during the summer while her friends
take glamorous vacations, fourteen-year-old Irene learns some lessons
about life after meeting a beautiful, yet troubled, girl.
ISBN 0-399-23784-4 (hc)
[1. Self-perception–Fiction. 2. Conduct of life–Fiction. 3. Interpersonal relations–Fiction.
4. Babysitters–Fiction.] I. Title. PZ7.G881325My 2006 [Fic]–dc22 2005013491

Speak Splashproof ISBN 978-0-14-240860-5

Designed by Gina DiMassi. Text set in Concorde Regular.

Manufactured in China

Foreshadowing happens in Epics, but never in real life.

In real life, I knew exactly what my summer was changing into—unrelenting hours of playing I Spy with Lainie Prior and telling Evan for the umpteenth time to wash his muddy sneakers, feet, or legs before coming indoors, while counting off the days until school started. Which would then begin a whole new countdown to the last day of school. I wonder when I can stop my countdowns? I guess not until the day I take off.

But I guess things could be worse. Five hundred years ago I'd be babysitting my own kids.

✳ ✳ ✳

OTHER BOOKS YOU MAY ENJOY

CONTENTS

I Am Fired

HERE IS MY DREAM. One day I am going to open my own beauty salon. It will be an upscale but cozy boutique in Los Angeles, with chandeliers and a white wood floor, where I will offer the latest looks. My specialty, however, will be re-creating the hairdos of Great Women in Literature.

I plan to call my shop Heroine Hairstyles.

In preparation, I have drawn seventy-six pages of heroine heads in my blue spiral notebook. Three heads to a row, four rows to a page, no order. On one page, Franny Glass is next to Antigone is next to Scout Finch is above Anna Kareni–

"Girl! You got shampoo in my eye!"

I look down. The lady's eyes are squeezed tight. "Left or right?" I ask.

"Who cares left or right? Get me some water!"

"I-*rene!*" My mom races from the cash register to the line of sinks. When Mom's mad, she says my name like it's a pronoun plus verb.

Rene (REEN): to perform an act of astonishing stupidity.

"Hurry up! My eye–my *left* eye–is burning!"

Mom has the hand towel and glass of water ready. She

shoos me off. Bella, sweeping up hair at the other end of the sinks, giggles while watching herself giggle in the opposite mirror. Working at a beauty salon is the perfect job for Bella, whose first love is her own reflection.

"Flush." Mom hands the lady the glass of water. "Apologize to Mrs. Conti," she hisses at me.

"I'm sorry, Mrs. Conti," I say. "It was an accident."

"You said the same thing last week." Mrs. Conti sits up, tips the water into her eye and blinks.

"A little water clears us of this deed," I quote. That's from Shakespeare, after Lady Macbeth gets her husband to pop off Duncan. It's not exactly an apology as much as an observation about how guilt can stain a person's character. Sister Soledad says I have a knack for ironic quotation.

Mrs. Conti looks like she'd have been happier with plain old groveling.

Mom signals Bella to finish Mrs. Conti's shampoo. Then she tugs me into the changing room, locking the door behind us. She begins with her usual sigh.

"Mom, I know. But I'm really, *really* working on paying better attention at the sinks."

"Honey, it's more than that," says Mom. "You've been here—what?—three weeks? And all I do is run interference for your crazy screwups."

"I'd feel better if you said honest mistakes."

"I'll give you honest," says Mom, "but let's backtrack a minute. In three weeks, you shrunk an entire wash load of fitting robes down to baby doll size. You put hot oil in the cream rinse dispensers and vice versa. You junked the magazines into recycling and left us without a scrap of reading for our clients. Then yesterday, you managed to mix up Mrs. Dent's color glaze so that her hair turned pink." Mom shudders at the memory. "And I lost count of how many times you've burned clients' eyes or scalded their scalps. People shouldn't equal an appointment here with *pain,* Irene. This is a beauty salon, not a dentist's office."

"But Mom, I'm still new."

"Three weeks isn't new." Mom is tapping her teeth with her nails. One coat of Cotton Candy and one of Rose Blush. I did them for her last night. I smudged a thumb but I don't think she's noticed yet. "Hon, I might own this business, but I answer to the customer. Don't you want to work someplace that fits you better?"

"I like it here."

"Yeah, I know, but . . ." Mom stops tapping and stares at me with those intense brown eyes I didn't inherit. "Maybe here doesn't like you back."

"What's that supposed to mean?"

Instead of answering, she hugs me. "I'm real sorry," Mom whispers in my ear, "but we've gotta eat and pay bills. Irene, honey, this is just not working out. I'm gonna have to let you go."

Something Turns Up

As I sit with my book on the hood of our car, waiting for Mom to finish locking up the salon, I can see and hear the epic of *My Life*, set to an evocative soundtrack.

What kind of mother fires her own daughter? narrates the brave, only slightly plaintive heroine.

My Life fades out once I get back into the ending of *The Color Purple*. At first I was reading it for Shug Avery's hairstyle, but now I have to see if Celie gets her revenge on any of the people who've been kicking her around. As a whole, this story puts a person in a kicking mood.

When I look up, Mom and Judith Prior are walking toward me across the parking lot. Judith owns the Plugged Nickel, a secondhand shop two down from Style to Go.

Mom is smiling. She does not bear the guilty countenance of a woman who has just sacked her own daughter.

"We have a plan," Mom announces once they're in earshot.

"Irene," begins Judith, "how would you like to come work for me?"

"Oh," I answer. "Hmm." Judith's shop would not advance

my future salon career, though it has its cramped, cluttered charms. There's a jukebox that plays tinny songs from the 1950s, and Judith lets her customers hang out all afternoon without inflicting any pressure to buy a single thing. I should know.

"What's the catch?" I ask.

"No catch," says Judith. "I'll match your pay here, plus ten percent."

There is a catch. Something twinkly is happening in Judith's eye. "What about transportation?" I'm suspicious. "And are the hours the same?"

"I'd come pick you up in the morning and take you home at night," says Judith.

"Why couldn't Mom drive me in, since· she works so close?"

"Because you wouldn't be working at my store. You'd be working at my house."

"You want me to babysit Lainie and Evan?" My voice squeaks. "As in, all day all week all . . . ?" The unspoken doom of *all summer* hangs like a bad smell in the heat.

"Lainie and Evan love you! You're their favorite babysitter! And we've been in a crunch since Dan's mom went back to Orlando."

"Let me think about it." Lainie and Evan aren't the worst kids in the world, but I couldn't imagine dealing with them regularly. Babysitting is a job that usually requires at least one day of recovery time.

"Beggars can't be choosers," says Mom. "Most other summer jobs are taken by now, and last I checked, you were too young to have a driver's license." Thanks, Mom.

"I hear the Lotsa Tacos over in Nutley is looking to hire," I say.

Mom snorts. I take her snort to mean there-is-no-way-in-hell-that-she-will-be-driving-me-all-the-way-out-to-Nutley. I'm not bad at interpreting Mom's snorts.

"Why don't you call me tonight after you've thought it over?" suggests Judith.

"I'll do that," I tell her.

I Do Not Get to Think It Over

MOM'S BOYFRIEND, ROY, used to be homeless, but for the past year or so he has lived at 711 Valentine Way with Mom and me. Mom likes the company of strays. Before Roy, there was Don the eleven-months-of-the-year-out-of-work Christmas tree dealer, and before Don came Bruno, a drummer for a band that had broken up before I was born. I have no idea what Roy was doing before he got dropped on our doorstep, but he seems happy enough about where he landed. He even cleans our house (not my room), does all the washing (not my clothes) and cooks us a hot dinner with bread crumbs every night.

I don't have anything against bread crumbs, but occasionally I'm not in the mood for them and then they annoy me beyond anything. Same as Roy.

Tonight it is chicken cutlet marsala in bread crumbs plus a salad.

"That's some look on your face," says Mom. She imitates it. Roy haws with laughter.

"I apologize if my mood accurately reflects my grim destiny, spending July and August babysitting the Prior kids."

"Gimme a break." Mom ladles a spoon of bread-crumby sauce. "You scored. There you'll be, out in the country, breathing fresh air instead of bleaching chemicals. Plus those kids are, what, eight and eleven? They can practically watch themselves."

"Babysitting is more than just watching the kids."

"That right?" asks Roy. "Like what?"

"Well," I start, "you have to deal with all this personal stuff. There you are, in another family's space, taking their phone messages and using their bathroom and–"

"Oh, please. Here's a job like a hundred-dollar bill lying on the ground," Mom interrupts, "and you're worrying if you can break it into tens or twenties."

I frown at Mom's imperfect analogy, but decide against commenting on it.

"I like kids," says Roy. "Kids say the darndest things." Mom and I pause to smile at him. Roy requires politeness. A tiny thing like not smiling, or smiling at the wrong time, can fly him into a rage. Like once when Mom asked him to "put on the water," meaning turn on the kettle for tea, and Roy turned on the faucet–when Mom and I started laughing, Roy went completely berserk and yanked the knob clean off the back door.

"Yeah, I like kids, too," I answer carefully–no mocking undertone, "but I might go nuts if I have to hang out in the boonies all day. The Priors don't even have a television. Anyhow, I'm sure there are other jobs."

"I'm sure there aren't," says Mom, pointing her spoon at me, "and tomorrow when I'm at work slaving away to pay rent while you're parked on your butt thinking over your career options, maybe the answer will become more clear."

"And remember, there's plenty of odd jobs around the house in the meantime." Roy winks.

The Epic of *My Life,* helping Roy bread-crumb cutlets while Mom checks in to see if I've done the laundry yet, suddenly flashes before my eyes.

The answer, suddenly, becomes extremely more clear.

I Receive an Impractical E-mail, and Then a Better One

AFTER DINNER, I check to see if any messages have arrived in response to my dilemma. The two I'm expecting did.

The first is from my best friend Whitney, who is spending a glorious, glamorous summer at Star Point Tennis Camp up in Stowe, Vermont.

The second is from Sister Soledad, who taught eighth-grade English at Bishop Middle School for thirty-five years until this spring, when she left to go live at Our Ladies of the Holy Trinity Retirement Convent in Cape May. I was in her last class. She said God couldn't have planned it better.

From: wlamott@starpointtenniscamp.org

Reeny!

What is that a joke? Babysitting? Repulsocity. Didn't you once tell me Lainie Prior pees her bed? I am weeping a thousand tears into my pillow for you. Guess what I got a belly ring! Mom said it was okay to get a piercing "so long as it wasn't nose or nipple." Ew from my own mother and it's still sore. A bunch of us all went in and all did it together and the guy who did it was such a skeeve but once it stops hurting it'll be so worth it.

I am getting way bored of Derrick and we've only been going out ten days! But there's another guy Kyle Ganzi who plays semipro and he is turning seventeen and hottie hot hot. Whenever he walks on court kids yell "Oh My Ganzi" but in a good way. I can't think of any news except our cabin's got this joke going where you end everything with the words "according to the prophecy." Kinda a have-to-be-there thing it's hard to explain!!!

Also I switched cabins so I'm not bunking with that weird chick Darlene anymore. Did I ever tell you about her duck underpants? On the back across the butt it said Cheez 'N Quackers! Sexy! Now I'm rooming with Grace who is cool and reminds me of Britta. Did you get a postcard yet? She was sort of bragging about her Dad's place with the pool and everything but what kind of techno-bully is he to not have e-mail access!? Going on Brit's postcard though Houston sounds kinda fun.

Anyhow I say: No job! Collect unemployment! Love ya!
—Whit

From: Soledad@olothtrc.com

Dear Irene,

Unstructured time out in the country, a place to read and sketch and contemplate . . . what an opportunity.

Oh, who am I kidding? That's the same junk Father Donovan fed me, and look where I landed. Farmed out to this glorified prison by the sea with nobody to complain to but six hundred squawking gulls and two hundred deaf old nuns. Irene, I am sorry your mother thinks you are bad for her business. But in your last e-mail, you had mentioned that you weren't overly confident that you were "cut out" (excuse my pun) for the demands of her hair salon. You had mentioned wanting to work more on the research and development side. So perhaps you should think of this job as a paying sabbatical?

Right now I am reading *Love in the Time of Cholera* and Fermina Daza wears her hair in "a single thick braid with a bow at the end, which hung down her back to her waist." Yes, another heroine braid, almost identical to Janie's "great rope of black hair swinging to her waist and unraveling in the wind like a plume" from *Their Eyes Were Watching God.* I suppose you had better stock your salon with braided extensions. I'm not sure our modern day world is as splendidly hairy.

Sister Maria Martinez, whom I believe I've mentioned before, has been giving cooking classes. Today I learned how to bake a mean banana bread. The secret, apparently, is half a cup of dark rum.

With affection,
Sister Soledad

I Take Fate into My Own Hands

LATER THAT NIGHT, I call Judith.

"H'lo?"

"Judith? Did I wake you up?"

"Irene?"

"Give me a twenty percent pay hike," I say, "and I'm yours for two months."

"Your mom fired you," she whispers. "You're not in bargaining position."

"I'll go work at Lotsa Tacos."

"Beth Ann would never drive you all the way to Nutley."

"There are other jobs. Lawn work and . . . um . . ."

"Twenty percent! Irene, are my kids that awful?"

"Every mother thinks her own gosling a swan," I quote.

There is a heavy pause.

"Fifteen percent," whispers Judith. "But you start tomorrow, and you can't tell Dan how much. Money's tight."

It's my turn to pause.

"Do you have a TV yet?"

"We've always had one. It's out in the barn."

"You'll need to put it back in the house. Otherwise, it's just too unfair."

"Fine."

"And I'm on the clock from the minute I get in the car."

"Okay, fine."

There is nothing else to say, and I am all out of nerve, and so I hang up.

A Beginning

BEFORE I COULD *keep up with it, my summer had changed,*
narrates my likable voice-over. *As for what it was changing
into, I had a feeling that it would be an adventure.*

Foreshadowing happens in *My Life*–style Epics, but never
in real life. In real life, I knew exactly what my summer was
changing into—unrelenting hours of playing I Spy with Lainie
Prior and telling Evan for the umpteenth time to wash his
muddy sneakers, feet or legs before coming indoors, while
counting off the days until school started. Which would then
begin a whole new countdown to the last day of school. I
wonder when I can stop my countdowns? I guess not until
the day I take off.

But things could be worse. Five hundred years ago, I'd be
babysitting my own kids.

Judith drives a purple Hybrid, which I think is pretty cool.
I don't know many adults who drive purple, earth-friendly
cars, or who, for that matter, have lucky colors. When she
pulls up to the house and I open the passenger-side door, she
presses a make-believe stopwatch. We smile at each
other. Truce.

She smiles again when she sees my new book, *Lolita*.

"How's the hair?"

"So far Dolores Haze has warm, auburn hair, but no hairstyle–yet. And her mom wears hers up, but I don't think she'll be a heroine of the book. Actually, I don't think this mom'll be in the story much longer."

Judith nods. She likes that I read a lot. She's not too into hair–she told me she cuts hers herself, and it looks like it, but she's always hopeful my reading sets a good example for her kids. It hasn't yet.

"Lainie still plays with those *Little Women* paper dolls you drew for her," says Judith, as if she's guessed what I'm thinking and wants to remind me that, while her kids might be illiterate, they are appreciative. "I'm warning you, she'll be asking you to make some more."

"Sure."

"And Dan dragged the TV out of the barn. The reception seems to be working if you do the ears just right. But I've laid down the law. One hour of computer or one hour of television per day, and that's final."

"Okay."

Then we are quiet. I watch humble Valentine Way scale up into elegant Clarendon Drive, and then we get onto the highway that will deposit me into the middle of nowhere. I feel my throat constrict. If only I could wake up tomorrow and be twenty-four instead of fourteen, and no longer have to count down the days until my real life begins. A quick note to Mom and I'd jump the first plane from Newark to Los Angeles, where I'd rent a garden apartment and host weekly dinner parties, regaling my guests with my chocolate martinis and ice-pick witticisms.

Judith has been talking. I tune her back in.

". . . because Dan and I don't want to be too strict. But we don't want the kids to get mush on the brain, either." Judith turns to me, heart-to-heart, as she pulls up to the house. "You know, Irene, I'm hoping that you might use all this time to sort of nudge Lainie and Evan. Creatively, I mean."

All this time. Like a prison sentence. "Uh-huh." I open the car door. "So, are they asleep?" Please, please.

"No, they're around back with Poundcake. We just adopted him from the animal shelter. Lainie tends to hug him too hard. So watch that."

"Yep."

"And no ice cream in place of meals."

"Right."

"Also, remind Evan that if he wants to take apart any alarm clocks or radios, he has to put them back together before we come home. If you decide to go to Larkin's Pond, use my bike, it's out in the barn. There's some pocket money for the Shady Shack on top of the fridge. Juice only, though. No sodas or foods with dyes."

"Okay."

I wave good-bye until Judith's car is smaller than a purple jelly bean on the green, neighborless horizon. I try not to think about Whitney on the grass courts or Britta baking poolside at her dad's bachelor pad in Houston, Texas.

The haunting soundtrack to *My Life,* a tremulous cello, almost moves me to tears.

Little Lainie

POUNDCAKE IS A thirty-pound bulldog with an overbite worse than Eleanor Roosevelt's. He is so excited to meet me that he throws up all over the kitchen floor.

"I'll clean it!" Evan runs cheerfully for the paper towels.

If I had known about the dog, I'd have stuck to my original raise of twenty percent.

I take the carton of soy peanut butter ice cream from the freezer while Lainie gets the bowls. Ever since I walked in the door, Lainie's fiercely adoring eyes refuse to let go of me.

"You grew out your bangs," she tells me. "Your hair's almost to your shoulders."

"Yep."

"I like it. It doesn't look as sticky-uppy."

My hand automatically reaches to smooth any lingering cowlicks. "Thanks, Lainie."

"Will you draw my new haircut in your notebook?" she asks. "Pleasepleaseplease?"

"If you want." Although Lainie's slant-edged bob makes her more pumpkin-headed than ever.

"Can we go to Larkin's later today?" asks Evan.

"Sure."

Lainie sits with her round fists in her lap. She has a way of waiting that's so intense, I can't finish my ice cream in peace. So I uncap my pen and flip to the *I.W.I.* section. "Hold still and do a fashion pose."

Evan looks up from where he's mopping up the dog barf and laughs. I reach down and cuff him. It's not Lainie's fault he's the cute one, with Judith's green eyes and black curls, while poor Lainie ended up with her dad's pale, wilting hair and uncooked-muffin face.

Lainie Prior's old hairstyle, an appalling shag, is in the *I.W.I.–Indulge Without Intent* index section. The creation of this section stemmed from a very awkward episode last year, when Britta's mom had badgered me about posing for my *Heroine Heads* book to the point where I finally had to break it to her that, as a rule, regular mom hair was just not inspiring.

"And here I thought my hairdo was so hip and jazzy." Ms. Gilbert had laughed, even as her eyes had turned all beady, waiting for me to relent. But I wouldn't, and consequently Britta didn't speak to me for four days. Hence the *I.W.I.* Artistic integrity is one thing, but when it starts to ruin friendships, then it's time to compromise.

Once my notebook is finished, I am planning to tear out all the nonheroic *I.W.I.* pages.

"Last time you babysitted us was March," says Lainie,

"and before that, two times in February, and one time last November. Now you'll be here evwy day."

"Don't say *evwy*," I say. "You're almost nine years old. You've studied the letter *r*."

"Mom says you didn't come back because we don't have a TV or good snacks like sour cream and onion potato chips," says Evan, with an impressive burp that he blows in Lainie's direction, "which is what all babysitters like."

"That's true," I admit.

"So then we had Mrs. Lupini, only we called her Mrs. Zucchini." Evan pauses for my unforthcoming laugh. "But, uh, she always forgot to turn off the stove, so Mom decided we were old enough to watch ourselves. Except last month Lainie ran away because she was one of the only kids in the whole third-grade class who didn't get invited to Gretchen McCoy's birthday party."

"Shutyourface!" screeches Lainie so loud that Poundcake starts to whimper.

"Well, it really happened!"

"So? It's private!"

"And then Grandma came to visit and she slept in Lainie's room, but Lainie peed in the bed—"

"I hate you!" Lainie makes a lurch for her brother and knocks over Judith's apple basket arrangement instead. Apples go rolling off the table and thud to the floor. Evan aims a kick at Lainie's knees and she gets a fistful of his hair. Poundcake increases his whimper to a howl.

"Lainie, let go of Evan, or I quit."

Lainie lets go. She looks blotchy and pitiful. Gretchen McCoy is obviously onto this.

"Ta-dah!" I show her my sketch.

"Ooooh!" Lainie puts her hands behind her back to show that she's remembered the look-don't-touch rule of my notebook. "You're the best hairstyle drawer in the whole entire world to infinity," she says, her voice solemn with certainty.

It's a funny thing about Lainie's compliments. While I always partly want to slap them off, they also make me feel so good that in the end I never do.

Some Cold Water

JUDITH'S BIKE IS a tired old fossil that owes half its weight to rust. We are hardly out the driveway on the way to Larkin's before sweat is trickling from pores I didn't even know I had. In spite of what my mother believes, the fresh air feels horrible. July is *Crime and Punishment* weather. Hot with a blanket of humidity to make you think you're going insane before you've done anything wrong.

I should check out that book again, for hairstyles. But as I recall, *Crime and Punishment* has mostly men and some prostitutes.

Evan ignores all that I tell him about bike safety, which actually funnels down to one rule—don't kill yourself. He does pops and back pops and skids and stands. Lainie pedals too close at my side and comments on anything Evan is doing that is hazardous or illegal.

If Larkin's Pond wasn't such an overcrowded madhouse of obnoxious kids, their scolding moms and the occasional growly dad, it would be great. It's very scenic. The water is enclosed by pine trees and divided by buoys. A large wooden dock balances the horizon. The few times I babysat the Prior kids last summer, we'd swim out to the dock and have dive contests. It was actually kind of fun, especially since Lainie was a good enough diver that she didn't end up in a snit or a sulk, which is the routine outcome of most of her athletic endeavors.

But this year, a wiser Evan knows not be seen anywhere near his sister.

"Zaps!" he hollers. "Zaps!" He throws his bike to the grass. At first I think this is some kind of dumb fifth-grade faux-curse word like *Zoiks!* until I realize Zaps is actually the name of someone Evan knows. The kid, Zaps, waves and Evan scurries off, ignoring my halfhearted reminder to join up with us for lunch.

Lainie wheels and locks her bike at the bike stand, then plops down stomach-first onto one of the two gigantic beach towels I've spread out side by side on the grassy bank. Something I've learned from last year's Larkin's excursion: define your territory.

"Go play," I tell her.

"But I don't know anybody here," she says.

"Go swim, then."

"I need sunblock."

Always something. I reach in the tote bag and toss her a bottle of sunscreen.

"It has to be the SPF forty-five," she says, "or I'll burn."

"You might have spoken up when I had the power to do something about it."

"It's fine." She pouts.

"What's wrong?"

"Mommy usually puts it on my hard-to-reach spots."

"You're too old to say Mommy. And I don't want to grease up my library book."

She sighs gloomily and uncaps the bottle, then rubs on white sunblock so thick, she looks like a mime. In my humble opinion, Judith and Dan Prior are doing a terrible job of equipping Lainie for the real world. She's way too clingy. Beth Ann Morse could show the Prior parents a trick or two. Mom let me babysit myself from age eight onward. By age eleven, I could make meat loaf and balance a checkbook.

Evan and Zaps are playing some game that involves two sticks and lots of yelling. I can tell it's bothering some of the other moms, but, oh, well, he's not my child. Lainie stretches out and hums, hoping I'll suggest a pickup game of I Packed My Grandmother's Trunk or something equally bleak.

Not happening. Avoiding eye contact, I roll onto my side and take out *Lolita*.

Then I see her. She is sitting on a high white lifeguard chair. Smack in the middle and opposite the dock. Hard to miss. But her chair doesn't need to be so geometrically centered, or so high. Her radio doesn't need to be turned on to KTZ All-Hits. She doesn't need to wear that Popsicle red bikini, or that mouthwash blue visor, or a swipe of bleach-white zinc on her straight, perfect nose. Most everyone is already aware of her anyway. The little kids, the older kids, the moms. It feels as if we are all watching her in our own ways. If any of us were asked to describe this afternoon, I'd bet money we'd all mention her.

I raise my book so I can stare more sneakily over the top of it. Who is she? She wasn't here last summer. She looks like a human but better, built out of more superior ingredients than skin and bones. Her muscles remind me of doctor's office roll-down medical diagrams, each perfectly separated and defined. It's hard to check her hairstyle, which appears short-ish, thickish and paintbrush black under her hat.

It's not like I never saw anyone pretty before. Lauren Corey and Tania Amarosa have been considered the prettiest girls in my grade since preschool. But they have nothing on this girl, who is hands down the most beautiful person I have ever seen in real life. The shock triggers my epiphany.

Nobody will ever stare at me the way I am staring at this girl.

It is the dead-honest truth. I will have birthdays, get my driver's license, receive my high school diploma and probably go to college, I will definitely leave New Jersey, but I will Never Look Like That. Ever. In the looks department, I will always be average. Average height, average foot size, average flyaway brown hair and average eyes an average color that everyone has seen a thousand times before. I've probably understood this all my life, but today, inside this electric moment, the knowledge feels new and cruel.

Then the girl blows her whistle. I watch as she skims rung

by rung down the lifeguard chair. Racing and diving into the water and then into a perfect freestyle. Wow, she's a really good swimmer. She moves so fast that she shrinks into a mini-lifeguard right before our eyes. Because we are all watching her, but it isn't until Lainie jumps up, screaming like she's been poked with a pitchfork, that I connect what the girl is doing with what's going on out in the water.

"Evan!" Lainie's voice is pure panic.

Only then do I pull back to take in the horizon, and now I see the spot of froth and foam. Evan? It couldn't be–*Evan!* Even as my mind clicks it together, the girl is already there, one long arm out, taking expert hold of Evan, flipping onto her back and hooking her elbow so that it picture-frames his face.

"Evan!" I shout, popping to my feet.

Other people are looking up, startled, and the next moment is mayhem as some of us dash to the edge of the water. I watch on tiptoe, my heart in my throat, as the girl smoothly, calmly brings in Evan. His eyes are closed and his body is sagging. My shock is like the ocean roaring in my ears. Was his skin always so zombie pale? Why isn't he moving?

"Evan!" I shout again. His eyes don't open. This is bad, this is bad, oh, this is so, so bad.

"Is he dead?" Lainie is running back and forth, her fingers sucked into her mouth.

"Space, space!" The girl half-carries, half-drags Evan onto the bank. She positions him flat on his back and drops to her knees beside him. Then she pinches his nose and dips her head to his face. Her lips press over his, before she turns and expels. And again. And again. My own breath hurts where it's sucked up in my lungs.

Finally, Evan coughs, jerking to life like Frankenstein's monster.

There's a spatter of clapping, a cheer, and everyone backs off a little—everyone except for Lainie, who flings herself face-down next her brother. "Oh!" she sobs. "I thought my very own brudder was *drownd-ed!*"

Evan squirms and turns away from her.

"Give him room," says the girl. "He's okay. You're okay, right?"

"Yeah," wheezes Evan. "Caught a cramp, no big deal."

"A'right, folks. Back to normal." The girl stands and waves off some of the younger kids. "You," she says to Evan. "Take it easy the rest of the day, huh?"

"Sure." Evan is staring at the lifeguard in awe and love.

She nods and turns to walk away.

I force my attention from her. "Are you really okay, Evan?" I ask.

His crooked-tooth smile appears on his face. "That life-guard is super, super hot," he whispers.

"Hey. Wait a minute." I sit back on my heels and scowl at him. "Were you faking?"

"Faking? Me? No way." But his eyes flicker and his smile is impish, leaving me in doubt.

"Ev," says Zaps, who has crept up on Evan's side. "Ev, did you think you were dead?"

"Only for a minute. I mighta felt my heart stop."

The crowd has dispersed. The girl is back up on her wooden throne, hands behind her head, watching the water in a way that now seems just a teeny bit showoff-y.

I approach the lifeguard tower. I feel like I should say an extra thanks, even if I also feel like a feudal serf, talking up to her. "Thanks for doing that."

She hardly looks down. "My job."

Her job: a beautiful lifeguard who knows CPR. My job: a dorky babysitter who has narrowly escaped a wrongful-death lawsuit. The girl squints out at the water and slips on her wraparound sunglasses. She wants me to go, I can feel it. "I'm Irene," I say.

"Okay."

"I'm that kid's babysitter. Evan. So if anything had happened to him today . . ."

"Then we'd both be out of work." She smiles grimly. Why didn't my teeth turn out like that?

"Yeah, I guess. So. Where do you go to school?"

"Thomas Edison," she answers. "I'm starting tenth."

"I'm starting there, ninth. I was at Bishop Middle."

She looks at me for the first time. "I'm kinda working here now, right?"

From the beach blanket I see Lainie watching, impressed. I wish I knew how to make the conversation last longer. All that comes to my mind is a quote from my Bartlett's about how silence is our universal refuge and the sequel to foolish acts. But this moment might not be the best time for a quote. "I'm Irene Morse," I say. Did I already say that?

She turns her head and looks at me hard. We sit in a painfully silent sequel to my foolish act. Then she says, "Okay." She puts some steam on the second syllable.

"Okay. Well. Thanks again. Bye."

Her hand ripples. She has already forgotten me.

I Have a Small Realization

THAT NIGHT IN my bedroom, I get out my manila envelope marked *P.P.* and sift through the most recent photos that Whitney, Britta and I sneak-took of Paul Pelicano from eighth grade Spring Spirit Day. His face is disguised by red and blue paint–Bishop Middle School colors–but seeing the photos gives me the same queasy feeling. Whitney calls it *being hot for* and *lusting after,* but I think the feeling is best described as *nausea.* Because I feel truly sick when I see Paul Pelicano, even in pictures. He is perfect. Long ago I gave up searching for his tragic flaw.

We've been taking candid snaps of Paul since fifth grade. It started as a joke, but the stack has accumulated to the point where we could reclassify Paul Pelicano as our friendly obsession. None of us has a visual eye, so every picture catches Paul in the throes of some bland act, such as standing in the outfield or waiting for the bus. Paul Pelicano, the face that launched a thousand stomach-cramping questions, and all of them starting: *What would you do if Paul Pelicano . . . ?*

Tonight, I would trade a Paul Pelicano photo for one

of the girl in the lifeguard chair. Just so I could look at her some more, to figure out what sets her apart from the rest of us.

Mom and Roy are talking on the other side of the wall that divides the bedrooms. Their voices have that out-of-tune sound that's not a fight yet, but has potential.

I refold the envelope and I think about the lifeguard girl, and I think about Paul Pelicano, the only person in this world I ever thought I could gaze at worshipfully all day.

Something thuds against the wall, rattling my lamp stand. Fight. I stand up to lock my bedroom door, since Mom has a habit of swooping in, post-fight, for a teary chat—without ever acknowledging the tears, or the problem.

I press my ear to the wall, but I can't tell if Mom is crying yet.

So I get in bed and open *Lolita* and turn up the volume of the words to block out the sound on the other side of the wall. There's no way this book is going to have a happy ending. Right from the start you can tell pervy old Humbert Humbert is up for anything. Here he's taking this girl, Dolores, on a road trip for the express purpose of slurping all over her, on and on about her round toes and her red, red lips and the way she chews gum—and all Dolores does is eat, which kind of reminds me of hanging out with Whitney, and then suddenly I really, really miss Whit, miss watching her loop mozzarella around her finger while we rank all the guys in our class from cutest to most repulsive, and I miss our Humbert-ish Paul Pelicano surveillances, and I wish that, for once in my life, my summer could have turned out to be better than hers.

Lainie Astonishes Me

BY THE NEXT DAY, I've schemed up a plan to ask the lifeguard girl if she wants to pose for my notebook. Although I can't think of a single occasion when I've asked someone to sit for me, I figure there's a chance that one of three things might happen.

1. She will be flattered that I've asked her to be my muse.
2. She will be impressed by my scrupulous, artistic attention to her hairstyle.
3. She will be astounded that I am familiar with so many Great Women of Literature.

Or maybe all of the above. All I know is that my notebook is my best shot.

"But I want to play Food Chicken," Lainie protests, "or Who Died in This House?"

"Tough luck. I want to go to Larkin's."

"Mom says I got too sunburned yesterday."

"Which means you tattletaled that I didn't bring the right sunblock. Thanks a lot, Lainie."

"I didn't tattletale!" Lainie squeals. "I didn't say anything! She *saw* my sunburn!"

"All right, fine. Stop crying. It's a beautiful day and you'll just have to suck it up, because Evan wants to go to Larkin's, too. Right, Evan?"

But Evan mumbles, "Food Chicken."

"Funny."

"I'm serious."

He's serious. I give him the dirty eyeball, but he doesn't elaborate about why he wants to stay in. Maybe he's shy at the prospect of seeing the lifeguard girl again, after their intimate moment of CPR. Maybe he's just being stubborn to resist my bossing. Either way, it's a pain, especially since Food Chicken isn't even that good a game, considering I was forced to make it up on the spot last year when I discovered there was no television to plunk the kids down in front of.

Lainie-plus-Evan, however, is a brat-force to be reckoned with. Or, rather, to not bother reckoning with. "Fine. Go get your money."

The kids dash upstairs. In the kitchen, I fill three glasses with water and set a silver mixing bowl on the table. Then I get the poker chips from the games cupboard.

"Handfuls for food, spoonfuls for spices, half cups for liquid. Dollar bets," I call up.

"Fifty-cent bets," Evan shouts down.

"That was last year. We have to adjust for inflation. And two bites!" I add.

"One bite!" shrieks Lainie.

"Two bites! New summer, bigger challenge."

The kids come bouncing down, Lainie shaking her fishtail-sequined purse and Evan lugging his iron mini-vault that probably cost five times more than anything he's got saved inside it.

We ante up. Lainie starts the game by tossing a handful of raisins into the mixing bowl. Evan adds his chip and shakes in some dry oats.

"Cowards," I tell them, and drop in a spoonful of horse-radish. We each eat two small teaspoonfuls of the mix, which tastes like spicy, uncooked raisin oatmeal.

"Second round," says Lainie, adding a spoon of sugar, which Evan scoffs at, but he uses his turn to pour in a half cup of water. When I squirt in some ketchup, the kids turn on their whine sirens.

"This is called Food Chicken, okay?" I remind them. "It's not called Let's Make Oatmeal Raisin Cookies. It's about test-ing your stamina. You play or you forfeit. By the way, that's very good advice for becoming an adult."

"Sugar's more of a cop-out than water," Evan mutters.

For round three, Lainie shakes in some frozen peas, Evan adds baking powder, and I finish with a half cup of soy sauce. I figure Lainie will call quits on this round, but she scrunches her face, holds her nose and gags her spoonful plus its encore.

"Nice form," I praise.

"Diss-*guss*-ting," she groans, but there's a flush of pride in her face. Unless it's the effects of the horseradish, which is making me feel a little hot under the skin myself.

Round four is a drizzle of honey, a handful of cornstarch and from me, onion powder.

We spoon it up. On my second bite, I get a frozen pea stuck in my throat and have to waste most of my allocated water to choke it down.

"Rrrround five," Evan calls.

Lainie hesitates. "Five chips," she says, "equals a lot of candy bars." She looks up at me. "But I'm *not* going to lose." She antes up.

"Big talk," mutters Evan.

"Pick your poison," I say.

Lainie looks like she might cry, but instead she hops up from the table, trots over to the fridge and returns holding an old, crusty jar of farmer's chutney. "Mom's had this forever!" She smirks at me. "You hate yucky old stuff like that, ha ha, don't you, Irene?" She opens the lids and sniffs deeply. "I remember you told me so when we played Food Chicken last year." She digs out a spoonful of the glop and plops it in the bowl.

"Well played," I say. "You're finally using some strategy." I repress my shudder.

Evan adds in some relatively neutral leftover macaroni and cheese. Both kids scream as I crack a raw egg. Lainie and I slurp it up record time.

It's Evan's turn and he freezes. Puts down his spoon. Then

stares at the lumpy, brownish pink stew. It is not an edible color.

"It's easier if you don't look," Lainie whispers encouragingly.

Too late. The horrendous mixture has its grip on him. That's a real pitfall of Food Chicken—if you're not careful, you can get yourself into a frozen-on-the-diving-board moment. And Evan's locked. He wags his head. "I can't. I can't do it." Scowling, he eyes all the chips in the middle of the table. "It's not worth it, anyhow. Stupid game."

"Well, I'm *not* going to lose," Lainie says as she spoons up her second mouthful, washes it down and wipes her lips with her arm. "Go, Irene."

I try not to think about that jar of chutney decaying in the Prior's fridge for Lord knows how long. At my second sickening bite, I feel myself waver. It's only the dread idea of losing to Lainie—and what an obnoxious winner she would be about it for the entire rest of the summer—that gives me the courage to swallow.

"Round six," I gasp.

Across the table, Lainie's brow is furrowed. I know she is doing her best to keep from crying.

"Time-out." Evan signals Lainie over for a private summit. Their heads bow together, whispering. "Good! Go!" He slaps his sister on the back as Lainie scrapes her chair over to the fridge and pulls down a tin from the top.

"Yummy, yummy. Christmas fruitcake," she sings. "This is the *way* oldest food we have in the house."

"Ancient!" Evan raises his knees to his chest and slaps his hand over his mouth.

"Primitive!" yelps Lainie as she trots over with the tin.

"Prehistoric!"

The smile I fake doesn't let on that I'm all but doomed. I hate fruitcake, even in its most fresh-baked attempt at Christmas cheer. The concept of eating it in July might just be beyond my human capacity.

Grinning, Lainie unwraps the foil and breaks off a piece, dropping it into the bowl in all its toxic glory. She mashes it up with the spoon. "On the first day of Christmas, my true love sent to me!" she screeches. Annoying as this is, I've got to tip my hat to Lainie for an unprecedented show of competitive spirit.

Unfortunately for her, that's why I have to make the decision to add in the dog food. It's a cheap shot—what is it about little kids' fear of eating dog food? I pour in the cupful of kibbles over Lainie's shrieking, wriggling protest.

"That's against the rules!" she wails. "You said it has to be edible!"

"It's edible to Poundcake. Two bites won't kill you. I'll go first if you want." I dip my spoon, close my eyes against the evil vision and swallow. The fruitcake sticks to the back of my throat, and I am pretty sure I can taste ancient, bacterial microbes. I gag and reach for my water glass, draining the last of my reserve.

Lainie is watching me in a state of gloomy shock. "Are you gonna puke?" she asks.

"Not a chance."

"You can do it, too, Lainie," murmurs Evan. "You can!"

Lainie's mouth is set. "I'm *not* losing from dog food," she says. And she tries. She really does. She plugs her nose and holds her glass of water ready. But when her chin starts to wobble, I can smell the money.

"You lost, you lost!" crows Evan in full turncoat mode. "You lost half your savings! Ha ha ha! Are you gonna be a cry-baby about it?"

Lainie's eyes well up.

"If you cry, he wins," I whisper.

"Then Evan wins *and* you won," bleats Lainie, "and I don't win anything!"

She's got a point. Anyway, there's no consoling her when she'd wanted it so badly. I sweep my eleven dollars' worth of chips into a pile. "And now I'm trading chips for the real cash. Rules are rules."

Lainie and Evan hand over their money with sad eyes but no argument. For a moment, I feel awful, and I contemplate giving both Prior kids their money back. But then I remind myself how easily they come by their allowance, and always for tasks like taking out the trash or making their beds. Chores that, in my house, Beth Ann Morse calls "pulling your weight."

So I decide that this time I'll take the cash, but going forward, I'll set a correct, babysitterly example. "Next time, we play with chips, for chips, and only chips," I assure them.

Evan bunches his mouth as Lainie wipes her nose on her arm. They both look pretty defeated. "Um, so are we going to Larkin's now?" Evan asks.

"Goodie! Larkin's!" Lainie hiccups.

Only I'm not feeling so great. I think I can still taste desiccated fruitcake in my molars. "I've got another idea," I say. "How about I just turn on the backyard sprinkler and we run through it and then go watch TV?" The sprinkler was a favorite diversion of last summer.

For a second, they don't say anything, and I really think they're going to punish me. Force me to get on Judith's three-thousand-pound bike and ride them over to Larkin's, just to spite my stomach's queasy churning.

"Yeah, okay. You don't look too good," says Lainie. "The sprinkler's around back."

"Let's do mud slides," says Evan. "We did that last year. Remember how you were the mud monster?"

"Sure," I say. How did I manage to scheme up so many activities for the Prior kids last year?

"Goodie! Mud monster!" Lainie is jumping up and down. Evan is already running for the door, and I know I'm off the hook. The Priors are sweet kids, mostly, and not too hard to please. Probably I don't give them enough credit for that.

I Am Slightly Slighted

JUDITH DROPS ME off at the town library so that I can restock. After everything that Humbert Humbert has put me through, I need a more sensible love story, and Sister Soledad has recommended *Jane Eyre*. Then again, she'd also recommended *Lolita*. I am coming to realize that Sister has eclectic passions.

I have to walk all the way home. Mom and Roy are sitting on deck chairs out back. They look fairly tranquil, despite last night's fighting. Good. "Hi!" I call out. "Yum, is that steak I smell?"

"Roy's grilling. But I thought you stopped eating red meat!" exclaims Mom. Code: None for you.

"I'm grilling chicken for you, special," calls Roy. Code: Don't touch the steak.

"Cool!" I call. Code: I am not going to whine about it. Whether Roy didn't remember that I'd switched back to eating red meat, or he didn't want to pay up for the extra steak—either way, it's not worth making into an issue. And Mom and I both know she can't give me any of her steak since Roy might be upset by the violation of his romantic gesture. Mom is Roy's mood-o-meter. She can detect the ghostliest signal that he is impatient or tired or has "low blood sugar"—Mom's pseudo-scientific "evidence" in defense of Roy's random personality swings.

"Real sorry 'bout the steaks, kiddo." When we meet up in the kitchen, Roy gives me a jittery smile that makes me jittery, too. "The chicken'll be up in ten minutes."

"Roy, will you choose some music?" Mom calls through the screen door. "You know I never pick the right tunes."

"You got it, baby."

I watch Roy trot over and start to fiddle with the knobs. He'll probably break it, he's so non–mechanically inclined, and that plus his temper is a lethal combo. Mom says I need to learn how to give Roy a chance, but how can I when he is such a ferocious composite of literary villains—Captain Bligh's weather-beaten face, Captain Queeg's beady eyes and Colonel Pyncheon's iron will, to name a few.

I can't imagine that my father was in any way similar to Roy, but I'll never know. Dad fell off a ladder and died of a broken neck when I was four. My memories of him are pretty vague, and are based mostly on times when he carried me—the giddy, sway-backed perspective from up on his shoulders or the safer hip-straddle, my nose buried in the cottony smell of his T-shirt. Aside from being my best mode of transportation, David Morse left me almost no impression, though I guess in the big picture, it's better not to remember too much, since then there's less to miss.

After dinner, Mom and Roy exchange the deck chairs for

the bedroom, leaving me a sink full of dirty dishes. Tidying the kitchen is always my job, but tonight it seems unfair, not only since I didn't get any steak but because our dishwasher broke last month, so I have to clean everything by hand.

Plus the air conditioner has decided to take the day off. I shove open the kitchen window.

What is it about the thin, slappy noise of water that makes a person feel so alone?

From the far back of the house, Mom laughs. I close my eyes and imagine Los Angeles, and how one day I will live in the middle of my life instead of wedged off to the side of it. In L.A., I'll have my own exactly right friends—not a confusing, jittery Roy in the bunch.

Suddenly I picture the lifeguard girl standing on a tropical green lawn, wearing a cherry red sundress, holding a chocolate martini and looking so L.A. perfect, so absolutely and flawlessly lifted out of my sunshine-splattered future that it seems to be a sign that my future can start whenever I want it to, if I want it badly enough. And right then, I feel it, aha, yes! I need to become friends with this girl as soon as I can! Yes! Of course I do!

No matter what she might have to say about it.

I Make the Acquaintance of Starla

THE NEXT MORNING, Judith tells me she'll be taking Lainie to work.

"You won't be bored without me, will you, Irene?" Lainie asks, clambering into the car once Judith pulls up to the house to drop me off. "You can use my bed for a nap if you get tired."

"Thanks, Lainie. You know I'd never nap on the job." I say this very loud so Judith hears.

As soon as they're gone and Evan and I have made ourselves bug-eyed from morning television, he asks, "If we go to Larkin's today, you think the hot lifeguard'll be there?"

"Probably."

Evan drops off the recliner and attempts a few push-ups. When he stands, his face is all crazy red. "How old do I look for my age? Do I look older than going-on-twelve?"

"Honestly?"

He frowns. "I guess."

"No, but you're a significant percentage cuter than Zaps."

This seems good enough for him. And so we're out the door ten minutes later, although nine of them are spent dealing with an upchucking Poundcake.

"Mom says he has separation anxiety," Evan informs me. "She says dogs are smarter than people, and they know when you're planning to leave."

"How's that smarter than people?"

Evan ignores me and rubs Poundcake under his slobbering chin. "Good boy," he says. "We'll be back soon. You just hang in there, guy."

The lifeguard girl is sitting in her chair like she'd never left it, except that today she is wearing a yellow racer-back swimsuit. Mom has always told me that yellow is "my" color, but seeing the lifeguard girl looking so perfect, I decide I'll never get near yellow again. It also makes me slightly grouchy with Mom, as if she's been duping me.

Thankfully today I'm wearing my best summer outfit, which is a composite of Whitney's greatest hits cast-offs. Over my own navy bathing suit, I'm in threadbare, low-waist tennis shorts, a striped tennis shirt with the logo ripped off, and sun-faded blue tennis sneakers.

"There's your girlfriend," I say to Evan when I realize that Evan is staring at her, too.

He looks sheepish, and then zooms off in search of Zaps.

I spread out the towels and take out *Jane Eyre* so that I can watch the lifeguard girl more discreetly. Plain Jane wears her hair in a meek little bun, but now that her rich boss, Mr. Rochester, is throwing himself a party, a few fancier hairstyles have turned up. The party takes its time getting going, and eventually the noonday heat is ablaze on my skin. So when the lifeguard girl breaks for a swim, it's easy enough to justify that this is exactly what I want to do, too.

She plows into the water like she's off to war. I plunge in to catch up.

"Hi," I say, too loud, with a big parade-float wave.

She ripples her fingers.

"I'm the babysitter from the other day," I explain, "when you saved that boy's life?"

"He was faking," she answers. "Kids do that." She snaps off her ponytail elastic and arches back to dunk her hair. When she comes up, it looks longer, sleek past her chin.

"The other thing I meant to ask that day was—I wanted to know if I could make a sketch of your hair." Then I add, so she doesn't think I'm too Humbert-y, "For this project I'm doing. My mom owns a hair salon. Style to Go, on Esplanade?"

The girl gives me a look like I might be a creep, anyway. "No, thanks."

I take a huge breath and sink underwater, pushing off from the rocks to swim away from her and out to the dock. Yuck, maybe I am a creep.

When I get to the dock, I'm winded, and I realize I forgot to put on sunblock. The day feels full of wrong turns, and as I make my embarrassed swim back to the bank, the sun beating welts into my shoulders, I take care not to look at the lifeguard girl, who is now standing in the shallow water, chatting with a couple of moms.

Evan has already attacked our pack lunch and absconded

with both sandwiches, leaving me a handful of peanut-butter celeries that have turned drooly-rubbery. I eat them and decide that even if this whole day is worthless, I'll compensate by asking Judith to drop me off in town so that I can buy some chocolate-pudding frosting, which Whitney and I like to eat plain from the can.

Back inside my book, Blanche Ingram is moving in on Mr. Rochester. Blanche is cuter than Jane, hair-wise, but I know Mr. R will eventually succumb to Jane's mousy charms because the author sketch shows Charlotte Brontë with a hairdo that is sympathetically similar to Jane Eyre's.

I wonder if Sister Soledad realizes that she's recommended back-to-back obsessive love stories, and if this has anything to do with Sister's own vows to Jesus.

A shadow falls over me. I look up.

"Hi."

"Changed my mind," says the girl, "about the hair." She sits down on the beach towel.

"Oh," I say. "Great."

"Since I'm bored."

I reach for my notebook. I have no idea where the lifeguard girl's head belongs. Not in the regular section. That's reserved for the Heroines. But not in the *I.W.I.*, either. On impulse, I open to a blank page near the end. I will put her all by herself.

"Will this take long?" She makes a haughty face as if she poses for pictures all the time.

"No."

"I'm off duty for half an hour." She points to her *Off Duty* shingle that hangs off the back of the chair. "On lunch."

"I only need a few minutes. Name?" I'm all business, my pen uncapped and hovering. The corners of my eyes are on watch for the threat of Evan.

"Starla Malloy."

There are names and there are fake names, and this name falls into the second category. Starla! Please. But I'm not in a position to call her bluff. I do a quick sketch. Her hair is on the frizzy end of the curly spectrum. Nothing special. It's not her hair that makes Starla amazing.

I try to look appropriately modest when I show her the finished result, but it's an exceptionally good sketch. I've caught the angle of her jaw and the sweep of her hairline. Starla barely looks. Instead, she holds out her hand. "Ten smacks."

"What?"

"Payment. For being your hair model, duh."

"I don't have ten dollars."

"Then you can bring it tomorrow."

I scrutinize her. Starla stares right back. Her eyes are a deep, caramel brown, thickly lashed. She is not joking, and I'm shocked to the core that she thinks I should pay for her sketch. "What if I show you the book instead?"

She shrugs. I hand over my notebook, violating my own rule.

"So what is this?" She flips through like it's a chore. "Who are all these ladies?"

"They're from books. They're a collection of the hairstyles of Great Women in Literature."

"Wow."

Starla's *wow* is one shade too close to mean. She starts reading my copied description of Blanche Ingram's hair. I can tell right off that she's no reader, out loud or otherwise. " 'Rich raven ringlets, a crown of thick plaits behind, and in front the longest, the glossiest curls I ever saw.' " She lets out a snort that would give Mom some competition. "Granny hair," she says.

"It's a complicated style," I acknowledge. "Not for beginners."

She tosses the notebook so that it lands on my feet. "No offense, but if you think people are gonna start wearing their hair like any of those ladies, then you've got yourself the dumbest idea I ever heard in my whole life."

"Any business that trades in pulchritude can be a lucrative franchise."

From Starla's expression, it's obvious she is not onto the word *pulchritude,* and probably not *lucrative,* either. Which was my plan. When someone insults you, I have found that the best thing to do is to answer with a handful of jumbo vocabulary. I have practiced this technique on Roy, so I know that it works. It's unsettling, and Starla's look is unsettled.

"Nerd!" she says. "Why'm I even dealing with you?" Suddenly she leans forward. "Touch my hair."

I feel strange doing so, but I reach out and give her hair a little pat. It's springier than I thought, and I immediately want to alter my sketch, although doing so basically admits I've made a mistake, which I wouldn't want to acknowledge.

"My mom is half Shawnee, half Irish, and my dad is mostly Puerto Rican, with one quarter African American, so I'm multiracial." Starla smiles as if she just won a bet against me. "What do you know about any hair that isn't your own? What hair could you give me that would be better than what I've got?"

I roll my eyes, because I know everything about all hair. Then I pick up my book and start turning the pages. "Okay. There's Tita in *Like Water for Chocolate*. There's Karana in *Island of the Blue Dolphins* . . ."

"Sorry, honey," says Starla, standing up and stretching tall, arms above her head. "I've got my own thing going. And since *you* copied *my* style, I should get paid, right? Ten bucks, tomorrow. Or the next day, or whichever day I see you. I'm not in any hurry. But you owe me, and if you don't make good on your debt, then I'll have to write you up in my blog."

With a final, sneery smile, she trots back to her chair. I watch her climb up and away. My heart feels like a bee landed inside it, beating and buzzing together. I roll onto my back and put *Jane Eyre* over my eyes so that Starla will think I have fallen into a nonchalant sleep. I want to hate her, but I guess I feel too unnerved–depressed, even. My first stab at a glamorous future has laughed me right back into reality. But who was I kidding? The Starlas of the world never become friends with the Irenes.

Affirmed and Reminded

From: Soledad@olothtrc.com

Dear Irene,

Your note reached me right when I needed a laugh. Not that I am making light of your situation. I can empathize with your shock at being criticized—by a stranger, no less—for something you are proud of. It reminds me of when Father Donovan warned me that as a teacher I "set a messy example" and that I needed "to cross my *t*'s and dot my *i*'s." It wasn't a harsh reprimand, except that being a teacher is what I am and always will be most proud of, and I'll never forget the thorny feelings his comments roused in me. Though I do think that if Father Donovan had known how deep his words had cut, he would not have used them.

Irene, I'm sure you still vividly recall last fall's Golden Bookworm contest, when you beat the 34-book record by reading 51 books. Remember when you got up onstage to accept your prize of *Bartlett's Quotations,* how one of your classmates called out an unkind remark? I watched you from the audience and knew your strength came from the knowledge that you had read every last book, and that your *Bartlett's* had been earned with enthusiasm and honesty.

All to conclude, you can hold your own against this Starla. Hers might just be an unusual friendship. In my own life, for example, Sister Maria Martinez can be very impulsive, but she always provides a reliable surprise. Last Saturday, for example, she rented a van and drove a dozen of us into Atlantic City for a dinner theater of *Cabaret*. Such fun! Never would I have thought to do such a thing on my own!

That old chestnut "live and learn" is not so tired a cliché when it happens in life!

Warmly,

Sister Soledad

I Make an Impact

STARLA HURT MY feelings more than I could let on to Sister S., but after Sister's e-mail, I decide to hunt down Starla's blog on the web. The search word *Starla* brings up a rock band, a scraggly folksinging trio, several sites dedicated to numerology, astrology and aura-reading, and then, aha! Starla's journal.

As soon as I'm in, I'm unimpressed. Horrendous blogs float all over cyberspace, and Starla's is not one of the worst, but it's bad. Shooting stars and music and loopy blue writing across the page:

> My Official Name Is Tara Malloy,
> But EVERYONE Calls Me Starla.

This might be the only sentence that doesn't contain spelling and grammar errors. Starla compensates for her illiteracy by accenting her prose with capital letters, exclamation marks and smileys. If I didn't know better, I'd think she was Lainie's age.

But I'm hooked, anyway. I click on photos of Starla's house, some close-ups of Starla's cat, Shadow, and too-many-girls-squeezed-in-a-bunch snaps of Starla's friends, who all look mean and sophisticated and confirm that gorgeous Starla is popular on a Paul Pelicano scale.

There's also a black-bordered link titled "Writings of D." These "Writings," when I click on, consist of a lot of dubious poetry about some guy, the mysteriously named D, who used to go out with Starla. She is obviously still battling to get over him.

> If you'd been Blue with me that's Bad.
> If you'd been True with me that's Rad.
> My Feelings you never meant to Hurt.
> My Heart you kicked into the Dirt.

I can't believe the same person who churned out a poem like this had the nerve to insult my notebook creations.

After a while, Starla's neon blog starts to hurt my eyes, and I'm just about to close up when I glance at her most recent journal entry.

> Today I had to do some part-time Modling!!
> Hey don't get the Wrong Idea that I'm Vane or a
> Sell Out–but Modling is lucrative!!!!!!!!!!!!

Lucrative. Even spelled right, which meant Starla looked it up and/or spellchecked it. It makes me feel the littlest bit smug, thinking that I made an impact on her after all. Even if

I wasn't mentioned by name, and even if our exchange wasn't one hundred percent accurately recorded.

Then I see a little ticker in the corner of her page that tells me I'm Starla's 776th visitor. That's three quarters of one thousand visits. More hits than the number of students at Bishop Middle. It's an impressive amount of attention, and while I don't want to be awed by it, I guess I am, a little.

The Morse House

THAT WEEKEND, WHEN the temperature smashes heat records, the implicit mother-daughter trust that prevents me from speaking up against Roy's "fix" on our air conditioner starts to crack.

"Even the Priors have a working air conditioner," I hear myself grumbling over my cereal, "and they're practically Amish."

"Shush." Mom looks nervously at the floor, beneath which Roy lurks in the basement, putzing around with his miniature battlefield diorama. Right now he's working on the Battle of Thermopylae. Re-creating battle scenes in miniature is Roy's other hobby, after clipping coupons and thinking up uninspired recipes and making (alleged) household repairs.

I walk up to the air conditioner, which is lodged in our living room's side window and is blowing in a sliver of cold air, a gale force of outdoor air and strange rattling noises. As soon as Mom retreats to the bathroom to get ready for work, I risk Roy's temper and clean the filters, which actually need to be replaced. This decreases the sound but doesn't do much for the heat.

Defeated, I collapse onto the couch and rummage for a snack from the collection I keep under it. Hark, a bag of chips. I eat them lying down, letting crumbs fall greasily into my neck, as my eyes race *Jane Eyre* to its mad, burning, blinding ending.

"See?" Mom breezes in. "It *is* cooler. He *did* fix it."

"Mmm."

"Oh, ye of little faith," she quotes lightly.

"Afflicted by love's madness, all are blind," I quote back.

"You know, Irene, you could help pick up this place," she retaliates. "If I work a six-day week, you should be able to work a five-and-a-half-day one, don'tcha think?"

"I thought the housecleaning was Roy's job." Though of course I don't risk saying this until a few moments after the kitchen door slams.

Eventually I defy my own inertia by getting off the couch, where I toss a few things into the sink, the trash can or the coat closet, depending. Cleaning up this place never seems worth the effort, probably because it's been the same all my life and, neat or messy, I can't see it any differently. When I get my L.A. salon, I plan to keep it immaculate, scented with vanilla-sandalwood candles and stocked with herbal tea in flavors like passion fruit or peppermint, which I will serve on doilies with paper-thin wedges of lemon. These details will become my signature style, along with my straw hat or light-weight cape that my exclusive clientele will find delight-fully eccentric.

I swoosh the couch afghan over my shoulders and glide into the kitchen to check myself out by the reflection of the toaster oven. Could I get away with a cape? What if I'd just been commissioned to do all the hairstyles for a big studio remake of *Pride and Prejudice,* and everyone is talking about the fresh and flattering looks I've created? I could pull off the cape if I could also successfully throw out comments like "You'll have to drop by the studio, darling!"

"Boo!"

I scream and jump. Roy, standing in the doorway watching me, nearly busts a gut.

"Oh, ha ha ha! Scared ya right in the middle of your play practice, didn't I–*darling!*"

Had I said "darling" out loud? A hotness springs to my eyes.

"Roy, just–don't," I warn him.

"Here I was coming up for a bottle of pop, and instead it's a Broadway show." Roy is doubled over. Under his T-shirt, I can see his stomach jiggle.

"It's really not that funny," I say. "You shouldn't creep up on people, it's . . . insidious."

"Sorry–*darling.*"

Of course Roy would have to kill his own joke. And I know it's an overreaction, but for a split second I'm so furious with him that I want to grab a kitchen knife and stab dumb old Roy in the chest so that blood comes spouting out like a geyser and he falls gasping to the floor while I stand above him crowing with manic laughter like Mr. Rochester's long-suffering first wife as I watch Roy's eyes cloud over with the realization–too late! too late!–that he should never, *ever* have underestimated my appetite for vengeance.

Lucky for us both, the insanity passes.

Instead, I stand frozen on my feet while a thousand potential insults crackle in my head. Roy thinks he has rendered me speechless, but all I feel is the yoke of Mom's restraining order. *Don't Upset Roy.*

But what if he is upsetting me? What about that? My eyes are pinpricks of warning, staring at him, as I make a pure, silent wish that he would just leave like all the others.

"Oh, haw haw! Oh, dang. Whew." Roy is winding down. He rubs his eyelids with the backs of his fingers. Still chuckling, he gets his drink from the fridge and toddles back down to the basement, to his Spartans and Persians. It takes everything in me to keep from locking him in down there.

Mischief

MONDAY MORNING, I learn that as a reward for Lainie's day of helping out at the Plugged Nickel, Judith has bought her a king-sized inflatable tube raft. The kids have already inflated it, and want to try it out on the water immediately.

"It's pretty cool that it's so big," I have to admit. "You could play a fun game with this. Like, maybe you have one person be Swamp Thing who tries to capsize the other two people."

"Yes, yes, yes! Evan can be Swamp Thing!" yells Lainie. "And we're both princess sisters, you and me, Irene. And we're on the raft and he tries to push us off, but also tell Ev the rule is no splashing water in my eyes." She wheels on her brother. "You splash my eyes like last time, Evan, and I will *not* forget to tell."

"Except for I won't be Evan, I'll be Swamp Thing, and Swamp Things have to splash. That's a rule, too," says Evan. Lainie looks skeptical, but stops arguing.

The bike ride over feels eternal, and the day is so hot and windless that with every passing minute, it's only the mental picture of myself submerged in cool water that keeps me going. Once we get there, though, I'm confronted with the even more powerful image of Starla, off her lifeguard chair and pacing the water's edge. It's hard not to watch her, but I deliberately do not. I spread out the beach towels and unpack the lunches and make a big fuss of coating sunblock all over Lainie's shoulders. Evan has already dragged the raft out to the bank and launched himself.

"Hey! Girls, get out here!" he yells. "What are ya, scared?" Then he starts making loud Swamp Thing-y noises. Starla shades a hand to look out at him before turning to smirk at Lainie and me.

"Come on," Lainie clamps her fingers around my wrist. She is surprisingly strong.

I yank away. "I never said *I* wanted to play!" All of a sudden, I can't bear the idea of appearing undignified while Starla is around, spinning on a raft with two little kids as if this is my top pick entertainment of the afternoon.

"But you promised! The game takes two princesses and one Swamp Thing!"

"All I said was three people *could* play. I was being theoretical."

"How about you come in after five minutes?" Lainie bargains.

"Maybe. When I'm ready."

Lainie's bottom lip sticks out, followed by her tongue. "Have it your way, then, meanie!"

I watch her skip off determinedly. The water looks so

blue, so fresh, that I can hardly bear not being in it. But if I go in for a dip, the kids will be all over me. So I stretch out and open to the first page of my next book, *A Confederacy of Dunces*, a Dan Prior recommendation that I found waiting for me on his kitchen table this morning, along with a friendly note from Dan about how it's his favorite book in the world. I'd never have picked up this book on my own, but I feel the tug of employee obligation. Also, Dan will be really happy if I actually do read it. And Dan is cool, right down to his baggy-butt jeans and the human rights bumper stickers on his truck. The few times Dan has driven me home from babysitting, I liked pretending that other people on the road thought he was my father.

So far, the novel is about a fat guy named Ignatius who wears a "green hunting cap squeezed [on] the top of the fleshy balloon of a head." The only hair described is what is sticking out of Ignatius's ears. From a style perspective, that's not promising.

I'd be able to enjoy the story more if Starla's presence didn't overwhelm me. Trying to ignore her makes my eyes hurt. But it's not until the kids are back on land, shivering and refueling on peanut butter and honey sandwiches, that Starla pivots in our direction and starts marching toward me. She has on her sunglasses and her visor is pulled low. She looks like someone who is famous, or at least someone who acts like she is.

Once Evan realizes that his dream girl is heading our way,

he leaps, choking on his sandwich, and runs off. Starla's life-saving kiss evidently has turned him into a lovesick idiot.

Her toes stop at the edge of the towel. "Got my tenner?"

I look up, pretending to be startled. As if I hadn't been aware of every step she took to get here. The speech I've been mentally preparing doesn't come out as breezily as I'd hoped, but I don't shy away from it. "If you'd mentioned in advance that you were charging a fee for that sketch," I begin, "then I'd pay up, no problem. But you didn't, and since that's pretty much the definition of a swindle, I don't think I owe you anything."

She is silent. Then she grins. "Nerd!" She shakes her head. "What, you think I need money so bad? You can have my picture for free if it means that much to you."

Which makes me feel extremely Humbert-esque, but all I say is "Fine."

"Anyway," she says through a yawn, "I'm on lunch, and I came over because I want to show you something."

"Show what?" pipes up Lainie.

Starla throws Lainie a sugary smile that most kids would find patronizing. Except that when you look like Starla, the rules change. "Don't worry about it. Guess what? We're going to Shady Shack. Ask your nerd babysitter if she's coming with."

"Shady Shack!" Lainie jumps up and pulls my arm. "Can we get some candy? Please, please?"

I really don't appreciate being called a nerd or a nerd

babysitter, especially because I doubt that Starla is being ironic. But to protest nerdishness pretty much dooms a person to that very category.

"I don't need anything from there. But if Lainie wants to go . . ."

"I want to go! And if I get some candy, you won't tell Mom, right, Irene? Right?"

"We'll see." I signal over to Evan, who shouts for us to get him cheese curls.

Shady Shack is set back in the pines behind the Larkin's Pond parking lot. It's bigger than a shack and no question it's shady, although better adjectives would be *dusty, overpriced* and *poorly stocked.*

Starla sails ahead of us, barely greeting the handful of admiring kids who are hanging out on the porch. One of them says, "Howarrya, Tara," which gets her a punishing stare. I guess not *everyone* has learned that Starla Malloy no longer answers to Tara.

Once inside, Starla jostles my elbow. "We used to go out. Look but don't look, got it?"

I follow her eyes to the kid sitting behind the register. Just by the way that Starla is breathing, I know this is D of the infamous "Writings of D." I'm surprised, because D doesn't look anything like I'd pictured—no piercing eyes and tumbling locks and gloomy, Mr. Rochester charms. This D is tall and skinny. He lets his hair fall in his eyes and he presses the buttons of the register with a single, hesitant finger—as if one wrong key might cause the whole machine to explode. He's an accidental, everyday hero. You could find a D anywhere. Working the pump at the gas station. Mowing your lawn. D as in *Dozens like him.*

"All through spring." Starla's whisper is humid in my ear. "April fifteenth through June twenty-first. And then *phhht.* School ended and he broke up on e-mail."

"Oh."

"He's really smart, brain-wise, but he's not all that hot, right? You wouldn't even look at him twice."

"I guess not."

"Right." But as soon as D glances our direction, Starla just about bounces out of her skin with the effort of not looking twice.

I nose around, taking a few more peeks at the mysterious D. The main interesting thing about him is the electricity he's charged up in Starla. She prowls up and down the aisles like a deranged cat, pausing to flick her eyes at D while pulling and replacing items from the shelves.

D doesn't acknowledge her. He keeps ringing up customers. There's a lot of traffic at Shady Shack, but I figure that's not the only reason D has not looked at Starla once.

"Can we go?" asks Lainie. "I made my pick. I want gum instead of candy."

"Sure." I buy myself an iced tea and a bag of caramel popcorn, a giant green Superblo gumball for Lainie, plus Evan's cheese curls.

"Hey," says D when he hands me my change. He looks up at me full-on, and I realize I was wrong. As eyes go, D's, in fact, could be described as piercing. They are long, almond-shaped and bright, silvery green.

"Thanks," I say back.

Starla, who has been watching D and me intently from her place in line, makes a squeaky noise, as if someone has stepped on her toe. I move on, quick.

When D rings her up, he says, "Yo, Malloy."

"Yrrmm," Starla mumbles. She keeps her chin tucked. In the visor and sunglasses, now she looks like a famous person trying not to be recognized while making an illegal purchase. When D drops her change into her palm, Starla makes a show of not wanting to let his fingers touch hers, which seems very immature to me.

As soon as we get outside, Starla claps a hand to her mouth. "Look!" She opens her basket-weave sling bag for me to see inside.

I look. I can't believe it. She must have stolen at least half a dozen candy bars. I also count four minibags of pretzels, two Lemon Fizzies, and multiple packs of chewing gum and Life Savers.

"You're crazy!" I whisper. "That's a crime!" My eyes dart left and right. I half expect the police bullhorns to start shouting for us to drop our weapons and surrender. "Why'd you do that?"

"Because of *him*, duh," she says. "It'll mess up his inventory like you don't even wanna know. Mrs. Hayes, the owner?—she'll definitely suspect him. She could even get him fired." There's a shine of sweat on Starla's skin. Her smile is as close to ugly as a drop-dead gorgeous person's smile can get.

"I got fired from a job once," I tell her, "and it was really humiliating, but at least it was my own fault."

Starla just laughs. "Stop looking up at me like that, okay? You witnessed, but I know you won't rat, right? Okay, my break's up. See ya."

She wants me to be more impressed, but what did she honestly expect? I search my soul for moral outrage, but the whole thing's just got me too surprised. Then I check to see if Lainie noticed Starla's shopping spree. If she did, she isn't letting on. One cheek bulges with bubble gum and her eyes stare blissfully at nothing.

Starla hops down the steps and walks away. Her weighted bag bounces low on the back of one thigh. I stare at the strong T of her shoulders and the lope of her brown, mile-long legs.

Lainie stares, too. "Hey, what'd she want to show us, anyhow?"

"Nothing important. How about you and I take the raft out now?"

"Yeah!" Lainie is easy bait. She squeezes my hand. "That lifeguard could win five hundred beauty contests in a row," she says, "but I like you being my babysitter much more."

" 'Much more' is redundant," I tell her, but I squeeze her hand back.

Two Postings

From: wlamott@starpointtenniscamp.org

Teeny Ireeny where are ye? I hope you're OK! You're not mad at me right? Have you forgotten all about your bestest pal?

OK nuff about you, on to moi. . . . Soooo it was hasta la pasta to Oh My Ganzi yesterday and now I'm totally loving Walt Waterman. Don't get me started on the name since his mom and dad must have been sucking on helium balloons the day they thought it up but lucky for him he is so awesome he transcends it. I'm not kidding. We had a barbecue last night and let's just say me and Walt also got hot and smokin'.

More on my love life as it happens . . .

As for other news: Big Mystery Hits Star Point Camp! Someone's been planting dead mice in the girls' sports bags. I am totally freaked but everyone agrees this joker's an improvement on last year's gift-giver known by all as the Crapping Bandit. Mia Whitbottom got moused 2wice so everyone suspects it's this kid Jay Crane who used to go out with her till she dropped him for Vasilii Gubin who's ranked #19 on the pro circuit.

OK now back to you—you haven't w/b since you were thinking about the babysitting job. Did you take my advice and chunk it? What are you up to? Living in a tree in your backyard eating raw lentils and protesting globalization or some other Ireney thing you've been reading up on is my bet. Britta wrote she hadn't heard from you either. I got another postcard—she's still in major love with Ernesto the parking attendant at her Dad's condo who a) doesn't speak a word of English b) won't give her the time of day and c) is like ten years older so what is she even thinking?

Anyhow, drop me a line and tell me how's it going.

t.t.f.n. (stands for ta-ta for now—how my roommate Grace signs off—so cute!)

Witty

The voice of e-mail Witty doesn't remind me of real Whitney. E-mail Whit sounds relaxed and happy. Real Whit is a diehard tennis fiend who is sometimes too quick to tell you about the vast importance of the warm-up stretch or the saturated-fat content of a granola bar. Ever since we became best friends in fifth grade, we've had the same straight-aim focus on our L.A.N.J.–Life After New Jersey. And a shared sense of suffering counts for a lot. But these days, Whit doesn't sound like she's suffering at all. For that matter, neither does Britta, whose last postcard reported that her obsession with Ernesto the parking guy left her almost no time to write. I've always comfortably counted on Britta being the least sophisticated of the three of us. But what if, come September, I become the odd one out? What if Whit and Britta decide I'm cramping their style? And, worse, what if they're right?

My fingers hover over the keyboard, but I'm not sure what to e-mail Whitney—mostly because there's nothing noteworthy happening to me.

It's like a galaxy separates us, and the name of that galaxy is called Whitney's Fun Summer.

After another minute, I move on to Starla's blog.

STARLAMALLOY'S JOURNAL

Payback can be so Sweet. Today I was feeling the Need to get back at D. This Need is Never far from my Mind. But risking Captchure I knew I had to be Crafty and Underhanded, right? Without giving up the Detales let me just say—my Plan worked!!!!!!!!!!!

This is not a Lie. I have Proof.

Who Ever is reading this, or even if U R not, U R the Secret Keeper!

You Are the Witness!

I reel back in my chair, stunned. She's talking about Me. I am Who Ever. I am the Secret Keeper and the Witness, of course, because Starla showed the bag of stolen stuff to me. This must have been the only reason Starla dragged me over to Shady Shack in the first place. So that she'd have her "Proof." Here I'd thought Starla was just trying to be friendly, but all along I was just a cog in the wheel of her Humbert-y obsession.

Why would someone like Starla want to chase after old D, who is also the one person in the world who seems wholeheartedly unimpressed with her? What does it mean? That no matter how flawless a person might look on the outside, she or he is always doomed to play the desperate Humbert, panting for someone else?

By that definition, does each and every one of us have a Humbert lurking?

Is there even some itchy old Humbert out there watching me?

I can't say it's an entirely disagreeable thought.

A Loss

IT RAINS THE next day, so Evan decides to hole up in his room and take apart various electronic fixtures. Lainie cuts me no such break. She digs out her best, ultra-point Magic Markers and forces me to crank out paper dolls at sweatshop rates.

"And then you can make a bridal dress," she commands. "After that, you can make a dress with sprinklicious flowers on it. Can you draw me a cat? And then can you draw the cat a nightgown?"

Finally I tell her that I have to finish *A Confederacy of Dunces* on her father's orders. "He's giving me a quiz on it Monday, so I only have this weekend to study."

"Yeesh, he gives me quizzes on my homework, too." Lainie's pale brow wrinkles. "Poor you, Irene. Even in the summer?"

I nod sadly. Sometimes Lainie is just too easy to fool. If only she were as easy to ditch. She trails me to the den, and then, after a few enraptured minutes of watching me read, she trots upstairs and returns with a copy of her own book.

"You can borrow this when I'm done," she says, waving it in my face.

"I'd never read that," I answer.

"Why not?"

"For one thing, there's pink glitter on the cover," I answer.

"That's so you know it's about a princess."

"And for another thing, I hate princesses."

Lainie laughs as she settles herself on the opposite side of the loveseat, her knees pressed against mine. "Sometimes you're a dumbo-face, Irene. It's against the law to hate princesses." She opens her book and sighs happily as I return to poor Ignatius and his world of mortifications and mani-festos.

Rain beats on the roof and the air is moist and clammy, making a perfect reading atmosphere, but my mind drifts to Starla, and what she might be doing right now. Did she have to slog all the way out to Larkin's in this weather? Is she sitting up there on her chair, monitoring some maniac swimmer with a death-wish-by-lightning-bolt? Are she and D the only two people at work today?

I imagine D slumped behind the register in the empty store while Starla sits out in the downpour, scheming up her next revenge tactic while also secretly hoping that D will stride out into the thunderstorm and sweep her up into an Epic-worthy embrace. Although on a glance, Starla's arms appear stronger than D's.

Later, Judith drops me off at a dark house. I hang up my wet Windbreaker and scan the fridge. Nothing. Nothing is on the stove or in the oven, either. Is it my imagination or has

Roy been slacking on his duties lately? Last week, we ate bread-crumbed fried mozzarella sticks three nights in a row.

A voice from nowhere says, "We'll order pizza."

"Mom?"

She's in the living room, all knotted up in Granny Morse's armchair. Something is wrong. For one thing, her hair looks terrible, and Mom never has bad hair days. At any given moment, Beth Ann Morse's hair is reliably clean, conditioned, blown dry, and anti-frizzled. As a walking advertisement for Style to Go, her good grooming is practically mandatory.

"Did you forget your rain hat?"

"I had to rush home." She shakes out a tissue and honks into it.

"Why?" It's not cold, but Mom has the afghan wrapped around her shoulders. "Are you sick?"

"Doesn't something feel different to you?"

I look around. Except for the fact that we are standing in gloom, everything looks the same. Is Mom protesting my poor cleanup of last week? No, she's waiting for me to notice something else.

"Roy's gone," she says, as if it were the most obvious thing. "He moved out."

I walk into the living room and snap on the lamp. Now I see that it's not just her hair. Other parts of Mom are looking bad, too. Her red-rimmed eyes, her rain-speckled shirt, the coral lipstick that hit only the general concept of her lips.

"What happened?"

"Beats me! A rough patch is normal in any relationship!" She blows her nose for emphasis. "How could I know Roy was so restless? He wouldn't even let me give him a ride to the bus station. He said the road was calling him."

Of course Roy would have to turn good-bye into country music. But Mom's sad mood is real enough.

"I don't know what to say. I'm really sorry."

She waves me off. "You never liked Roy."

"Well, but that doesn't mean I'm not sorry."

"Get us a large, with anything but mushroom, okay? There's money in my wallet."

I try to think of a comforting quote. "A roving heart gathers no affection."

Sadly, Mom has never been receptive to a Bartlett, no matter how fitting. "And order us a salad, too."

"Okay." Suddenly I remember back to my wish that Roy would just leave. I am not superstitious by nature, but the coincidence sends a twinge of guilt through me. "So I'll be in my room," I say, "if you want to talk or something? I won't lock the door."

She nods. Her head droops like her battery is dying. I snap off the lamp. I figure the internal soundtrack to Mom's life, most likely a mellow, acoustic guitar, sounds better in the dark.

A Greater Loss

"My hairstyles notebook is missing."

The kids look up from their bowls of breakfast ice cream.

"Are you sure?" asks Evan. "When was the last time you saw it?"

I calculate back. I hadn't been using the notebook since last week, when I started reading *Dunces*. Then on my Saturday trip to the library, my favorite librarian, Miss Kitamura, had presented me with a book called *Obasan*.

"I've been holding it especially for you, Irene, since you're my best reader," she said. As hairstylishly unpromising as it had looked, I accepted it, my dilemma being that Miss Kitamura is Japanese and *Obasan* is by a Japanese author, and to refuse to take it seemed a personal snub against Miss Kitamura, who had helped strategize my Golden Bookworm victory with her many excellent recommendations.

Then I ended up reading *Obasan* in the library all day to avoid being at home, where Mom kept calling in every five minutes to check if I'd heard from Roy.

Unfortunately, now *Obasan* won't let me put it down until I find out the secret of where Naomi's mother ran off to.

"That notebook is always, always in my bag." I rummage through it again.

"Not always-always. You left it like fifty different places in the house last week," Lainie reminds me. "You were using the back of it while we were doing paper dolls. But I'll go check and see if it's upstairs." She scampers off.

"Nope!" she calls down five seconds later.

"Look harder!" I shout up.

"Can I go ride bikes with Zaps?" asks Evan.

"Nobody's going anywhere until we find my notebook," I tell him. "We're going to take this whole place apart."

For Lainie and Evan, taking the whole place apart really means throwing around the couch cushions and banging cupboards so the end result looks as if someone lifted the house off the ground and shook it like a snow globe. I'm not sure how much actual searching is accomplished, but in times of frustration, the banging is usually the point. I rattle drawers and slam closet doors. My stomach is getting squeamish. Where could I have left it?

"Maybe it's at your house?" asks Lainie.

"Maybe. I don't know." I press my palms to my eyes, trying to Visually Project, like in that news story I read about police psychics. My Visual Projection is a melted ice-cream puddle of Larkin's and sunshine, bike rides and books, Starla and paper dolls. "I guess it could be anywhere."

"I need to finish my breakfast before I start looking again." Lainie zips off to hide in the kitchen.

Evan and I bang around a few more minutes before he gives up, too. "It's just a lame-o doodle book, anyhow," he huffs. "I don't see what the big deal is."

I whirl on him. "The big deal is it's my future business!"

"Well, if you want my opinion," Evan says loftily, "you're not the right person to be a small-business owner."

"That's not your opinion!" Lainie shouts from the kitchen. "You're only copying what Mom said about Irene last night!"

"What?" Picturing the Prior family discussing me over the dinner table is a really bothersome image for me, which isn't lost on Evan. His eyes get big and round.

"No, all I . . ." Evan backs off me a step. "Mom was just saying . . . I mean . . . hey, don't look at me like that, Irene, okay?"

"You don't trust I could do what your mom does? Or *my* mom? You think I'm not as capable as either of them?"

For a second, I think Evan might turn and bolt upstairs, but he holds his ground. "Be mad if you want, but didya ever notice how Mom acts in her store? How she can remember eighty-six things all at the same time? The nuts and bolts, Mom calls it." He twists his mouth, scrutinizing me. This expression makes him seem wiser than his age.

I know what Evan's getting at, but I refuse to make it easy for him. "You don't think I'm a nuts-and-bolts person?"

He pauses, then plunges. "No. You're more of a sit-around person."

"Okay, so basically you're telling me that I'm *lazy*?"

"Not lazy, just—you know how you are, Irene. How you sit doing those ladies' heads and you don't hear if Poundcake's scratching to come in or notice other stuff going on around you."

"Evan," I begin, "that notebook is my research. I don't draw heads to amuse myself. I draw heads because I have to."

"You're taking this as an insult, and that's not how I mean it," says Evan.

It's true and he's right. In the back of my mind, I fear Judith's job. And Mom's. The nuts and bolts of Style to Go got me in trouble. *Fill the shampoo dispensers, sweep up the hair, fold the towels, show Mrs. Gonzales to the changing room.* It was too much to keep track of, my mind would get scrambled and inevitably I'd make a mess, just like poor, fat Ignatius—only his loving mother didn't thwack him with the back of a hairbrush every time he screwed up.

"So what did you all decide I should do with my life?" I ask.

"Start a paper doll company!" hollers Lainie.

"Mom thinks you'd make a good teacher," says Evan, "if you put your mind to it."

"And Dad says you have the right concentration for being a lawyer!" Lainie shouts. "But only a lawyer for public defense, like him. Not the kind who has yachts."

"Gee, thanks. Tell your parents I'm glad to come in so

handy as a subject of debate . . . " My voice drifts off, because my tone shames me, especially since I'm pretty sure I once read a Bartlett quote about sarcasm being the lowest form of humor. Even though my future is always an extremely interesting topic to me, it feels strange to be noticed by the Priors, and I'm not sure how much I like the sudden spotlight.

A Small Reprimand

From: wlamott@starpointtenniscamp.org

Ireney-bean,

Carrie my doubles partner is starting to call you my "friend" with quotation marks around it because she thinks I'm making you up. That would be on account of you *never* e-mailing which consequently results in me *never* having *any* news about you.

Maybe I am making you up?????

But I will keep writing you because I am that kinda pal. Sooo . . . Walt Waterman and me are still Love-All. That's a little tennis humor for ya. On a recent excavation of his superfine bod I discovered a tat of a snake on his thigh and another on his shoulder of a broken heart. He got the snake with his best friend Dingo but he won't tell me about the heart only gets a mystical look in his eye and says it's complicated. When W.W.'s not being mystical & complicated he's the funniest guy at camp—in that scary way that makes you glad you're on his team. Choice Walt lines: "Let me translate that into moron for you" and "I didn't realize you were fluent in clueless." But it's more the way he says it—kinda gotta be here . . . and I kinda wish you were here even if you claim tennis gives you heat rash.

Drop me the news or give me 1 good reason why you won't. What'd I ever do to chafe?

t.t.f.n.

La Whit

I have zilch to report to Whitney so far, but I know that if I don't write my best friend very, very soon, I'll be in deeper trouble than anything my bargaining skills can navigate.

So I hit Reply, take a breath and go for it.

Whatsup Whitty-whitpecker——

Wow do I get the Neglectful Friend Medal or what ??? but so much is Up——the Prior job is paying me big $$$ and I met this girl Starla who is the coolest and we've been hanging out. Last nite we met up with these two awesome guys in the Lotsa Tacos parking lot——Matt and Lars——surfers visiting from Malibu Beach!! I got together with Lars after——

My fingers stop. Who am I kidding? Even my most brave and vivid flare of imagination starts to sputter when attempting to picture myself hooking up with some random surfer dude named Lars in a fast food parking lot.

I send my cursor chomping backward and try again.

Whitly——

Sounds like you are having an amazing summer. Lucky you to get to go tennis camp, and here I can't even afford a tennis *racquet! So much for justice in this world. Some of us get bonfires and sing-alongs, others are resigned to the grim fate of the downtrodden, underpaid for overtime and nothing to——*

Nope. I delete that one, too. I stare at the blank message Reply space, hypnotized by my inability to spin my summer into anything that sounds remotely fun, and feeling a touch sorry for myself that I have so little news to work with at all, until the sound of the front door unlocking snaps me from my trance. It's Mom, with our Chinese takeout dinner.

Which makes it easier to decide that I'll tackle the Whitney write-back issue on a full stomach of egg rolls and shrimp fried rice.

A Bad Angel

THE NEXT DAY, it's Evan's turn to go work at the Plugged Nickel. "I do the inventory, since I'm gifted at math," he tells me, his chest puffed out like a superhero. Though he has absolutely improved from last summer, there's still a good chunk of dork left in ole Evan.

But Judith doesn't seem to mind or notice. She reaches out and rumples his hair. "Say, Irene, you should ask your mom to hire Ev. She's always talking about the chaos in her stockroom."

I don't answer. I'm still on guard about the Priors deciding that I'd be an unwelcome addition to the world of small-business owners. Now it seems to be Mom's turn under the Prior spyglass.

When Lainie and I ride out to Larkin's, I make her work hard to keep up. Judith's comment has annoyed me.

"Jeez McCheese, I'm happy you don't ride Evan's bike every day!" puffs Lainie as we lock them at the stand. " 'Cause you sure are a fast bike rider! I bet you could win that big ride they put on television."

"The Tour de France."

"Yeah, I bet you'd clobber."

"I'll go slower on the ride home." It's not fair to take my petty grudges out on Lainie. I open a juice pouch and give it to her to rehydrate.

Starla stands leaning against her chair, her chin uplifted, hands resting lightly on her hips, watching the water like a supremely bored sea captain. I'm coming to realize that there's something slightly unnatural about how Starla expresses and arranges herself, as if she knows about all the attention people are beaming onto her—even when she isn't doing a thing. Being too eye-catching must be slightly exhausting that way.

Lainie trots right over. I follow. I haven't seen Starla since last week's junk-food theft. I was half imagining that she'd have been caught by now. Also arrested, and put on probation, and held up by local Larkin's gossipmongers as an example of Teenage Delinquency.

"Where were you the other day?" asks Lainie. "Me and my brother came here with our parents and you weren't around."

Starla smiles down at her. "Even lifeguards get weekends off, cutie-pie."

"You should come back to our house for lunch. Since Evan's not around to ruin everything."

"Uh-huh," answers Starla.

"We're the last house on Highland and we've got three acres. That's enough land for a pony but I'm not allowed one."

"I'll stop by some other time," says Starla in a flat voice, her eyes cutting at me in warning that Lainie's thin charms have worn out.

Lainie, deaf and blind to all social cues, touches the leather strap bracelet on Starla's wrist. "That's pretty."

"Did you get that in Idlewild?" I hadn't meant to blurt this—but I'd logged on to Starla's journal yesterday and learned that she and some of her friends—*Me + Kelli + Em = FUN!!!*—had hit the mall. I'd even checked out the photos: of long, rangy Em drinking a soda and crossing her eyes at an indoor mall café; of wispy blonde Kelli plus Starla imitating the mannequins' poses in a lingerie storefront, and then one of all three, the camera held out and tipped so you could see up way too much nostril. I'd tried to cipher from the photos if Em and Kelli, as the cute-ish friends of gorgeous Starla, understood what they were up against. Did they huddle together or whisper on the phone about how all the guys loved Starla best? Did they despise Starla for her power? Or were they in constant competition to win her favor? Or maybe I was stone wrong, and Kelli and Em were perfectly at ease about their pal. That's what their blandly happy smiles seemed to be telling the world—though photos often lied.

Now I quake in horror, having exposed myself to Starla as a lonely blog-haunter and creepster. I am speechless with embarrassment.

Starla snaps her fingers. "Gotcha, Nerd! I knew you'd go on my journal." She looks genuinely delighted. "Did you read my poems, too?"

"I might've read a couple . . ." I hate when Starla calls me Nerd, and Lainie's bat-eared presence makes me doubly uncomfortable. I point. "Hey, Lainie, don't you know her?"

"Annie Waldron?" Lainie glances over at the freckly girl sitting under a tree, pretending not to notice that her mother is braiding her hair. "She's in my class."

"I thought so." I shove her. "Go say hi."

"But Annie Waldron is icky."

"How?"

"She just *is*."

"But now she saw you, so you have to go. It's the polite thing."

Lainie's shoulders sag. "Only because you're making me, not because I want to. And it's not like you're so polite, Irene. How many people are *you* making friends with around here?"

"That's my business," I say, squaring her by the shoulders and pushing her off.

As soon as Lainie's out of the way, Starla flips her *Off Duty* shingle. She trails me while I pick a spot on the grass and spread out the towels. Lainie's comment has embedded itself in my brain, and I smile in what I hope is a friendly and outgoing manner. Starla does not smile back. "So, Nerd, just between us," she says, "tell me what you think of my poems. For real."

I weight the corners of the towel with rocks. "First, stop calling me Nerd."

"Just admit it that I'm good at rhymes. My friends all say so."

Then I have an idea. *Obasan*, which I finished yesterday, is still in my bag. "Listen to this." I flip to a place and read. " 'The stillness is so much with me that it takes the form of a shadow which grows and surrounds me like air.' " I look up. "The girl is talking about missing her mom. There's more poetry in that sentence than in something like 'My mom's not here, she's gone I fear.' "

"*Your* opinion." Starla makes a face. "It's not even in a regular poem shape."

"It's not supposed to be."

"You can't just read some mushy sentence out of a book and call it a poem."

"But that's my point. Poetry doesn't have to–"

"Because I can make any word rhyme. Go ahead. Pick a word."

I replace *Obasan* in my bag. "Braggart."

"Ha, nice try." Starla glares at me like she's the sheriff and I'm the sneaky outlaw. "That's not a word."

"It is, too. I promise."

"All it rhymes with is *fart*."

"That's only approximate rhyme, and if you're going for that, a better choice might have been *swagger*. Or *laggard*."

Starla's glare tightens by a notch. "You're pretty conceited. You think I can't tell the difference between real and made-up words? You think I'm stupid, right? You and D, you both do. But I've got stuff going on up here all the time." She taps her temple. "Sometimes I get dizzy from all the things in my mind. No joke." Her voice gets louder. "All you nerds are alike. You act like you're the only people who think. And mostly what you're thinking about is how you're better than everyone else. But you're jealous of me, too. I know. I see how you watch me."

"I don't think I'm better than you, and I definitely don't watch you," I say. It surprises me that Starla could possibly care what I think.

"Come watch what I do next, *Nerd*." Starla turns and starts walking. "I'll show you something," she calls. "Something worth watching."

And then I have to follow her, because her anger is so purposeful.

"I can't stay away too long. I need to keep an eye on Lainie," I say to Starla's back.

She waves me off. "There's sixty moms on patrol today. Chill."

So I trail her all the way to the parking lot, where Starla stops in front of a small, shiny blue car. If Starla had magical powers, the look she gives this car should have caused it to explode.

"D took me out in this." She kicks at a dinged hubcap.

"We went out a lot of times. You think you're so smart, tell me why someone would go out with you and then break up for no reason as soon as school ends?"

"Maybe it wasn't about you."

"Oh, shut up. I can get an answer like that out of any magazine." Starla moves close into my space. "We did stuff in this car, you know? And every time I see it parked out here, I *feel* it all come back to me. Sometimes I feel it too much." She presses her heart. "That's why poetry is cool. I can explain my life a thousand times better in poem form."

Under the hot sun, the faint line that traces above the shape of Starla's upper lip seems exceptionally pale, X-ray lit, against her tan skin. Or maybe I just noticed this, the way I'm always noticing new colors and angles of Starla. The smile she gives me is a duplicate of the smile I saw after she robbed Shady Shack, and my muscles tense in anticipation of whatever next trick she's got up her sleeve. Then she fishes something out of her pocket.

It's a key, swinging on a loop of soft twine.

I look around, trying to figure out what she wants to unlock. Nobody else is in the parking lot. The couple of kids lolling on Shady Shack's porch to beat the heat have their backs to us.

But Starla doesn't unlock anything. She slashes the key across the car door's paint. It leaves a dark scratch.

"Wait! Stop!" I make a grab for her wrist and she snatches it away.

"You don't feel how I do when you see this car," she says. I hear the rasp of metal on metal as the key's edge digs deep and fierce. The scar she leaves in her wake is like the claw mark of an animal. She walks around it, slow, taking her time.

I step back. I step back again. I can hardly breathe, but I can't stop watching.

Once Starla has returned to the point where she started, she pauses. Her breath is shallow. She holds up the key. "D, who took away our Love," she intones, "Wise and Perfect as a Dove." She's quoting her own appalling poetry.

"Starla, it's not a crime to break up with someone," I say. "But you—you've robbed this guy's store, and now you've messed up his car. Those are crimes."

"You can't judge me. You've never been in love." Starla reaches over, bringing the point of her key to the underside of my chin, and for a half second I wonder if she's going to scratch me, too. I don't speak, I don't move, even my lungs seemed to have stopped functioning. Starla holds my eye. Then she pockets the key. "When you're in love, when you want to be with someone so much that you'll go with that person anywhere, you'll ride in his car and let him drive you where he wants and let him touch you where he wants and do what he wants and then he has all that . . . *information* about you, to tell his friends or whatever he wants to do with it— that's a crime, too, okay?"

I try to imagine D telling his friends all the secret details of Starla. About where her hidden moles are located and if she's got bikini rash or bad breath. And while D doesn't seem to be the type to gossip, I guess that's not the point.

"Call it a tie now," I tell her. "Because now you have information, too. You know who robbed Shady Shack. And you know who messed up his car."

She smiles. It's a sad little-girl smile. "And you know it, too, right? You're my Witness."

"Exactly."

"Because if I didn't have you watching, it's like it didn't happen."

"It happened, I promise."

This seems to relax her. Now she looks around, as if she's just remembered where she is. "Y'know, every time I put on my *Off Duty* sign, one of those moms complains. No joke. Every single time. What, I can't even go to the bathroom?" She wipes her shiny forehead with the back of a hand. "I need a cold drink. Come with me." She eyes Shady Shack. And I know what she wants to do. She wants to gloat, to waltz and loiter up and down the aisles, stealing looks at D, making him uncomfortable, enjoying her information.

"Actually, I brought juice pouches," I say. "Shady Shack's so overpriced."

"Ha, I can get you a discount." Starla winks.

I haven't done anything wrong, of course, but even sharing this laugh with her makes me feel guilty.

Longing and Disappointment

STARLAMALLOY'S JOURNAL

D, there are Rumors that you are Free of Me. I am Happy for you. I want you to be Free. But. Know this: Freedom has its Price.
A Heart that Beat for you,
Still Beats with Love
Without You.

The poem doesn't rhyme, and yet it retains the distinct Starla quality of being terrible.

I log off and pick up Sister Soledad's note.

From: Soledad@olothtrc.com

Dear Irene,

I'm sorry not to have written you back promptly, but I've been a bit down in the dumps. Recently I have learned that Sister Maria Martinez has requested to be reassigned to Sisters of Saint Luciana, a convent right outside Lima, Peru. She has family there, and she leaves in less than two weeks.

It is impossible to think about this house without Sister Maria inside it. She is the heart and soul and life of the Holy Trinity. She brightens up every room she's in.

Don't be too upset with Whitney's presumably perfect days at tennis camp, or Britta's summer in Texas. And don't be upset that you are resentful. Envy is, alas, a natural condition. I am recommending *Tender Is the Night* as a story about people who on the surface seem to have everything. It also has those inimitable Jazz Age hairstyles.

Fondly,
Sister Soledad

Sister's S's note is more personal than I am used to. I never think of Sister S as "down in the dumps." I've never thought about her emotions, period. She is, after all, a nun.

I try to picture Sister's life as an Epic, set to a soundtrack of organ music. I imagine dozens of creaky sisters on creakier rocking chairs on the creakiest wraparound porch in Cape May. Then I stop. It's too dismal. Sister S's life is not a movie I'd go see, or a book I'd pick up. But Sister Soledad shouldn't be sentenced to the rocking chair—not yet, anyhow. She's too lively. Her eyes are like silver marbles that could confuse a person into wondering if she's a crazed religious zealot or a soothsayer, but she's neither. She's just curious. Every year, Sister pieces and sews a quilt using scraps of material donated from each of her English students. She's traveled to Yosemite with Bird Quest. She roots for the Knicks over the

Nets. She Irish step-danced for the March of Dimes at Bishop Middle's Spirit Day. Sister's lots of things, and she's also shy. Not that she ever admitted such a thing, but you could always hear it when she had to make announcements at morning assembly, how she'd breathe too hard in the microphone, then scurry from the podium while kids still had their hands raised.

So when Sister Maria Martinez came bouncing around the creaky corner of that wraparound porch with plans for a night out in Atlantic City, I'm sure Sister Soledad's pale eyes flared like sparklers. She loves new things and fun things and anything that makes her laugh.

It's been a while since I felt truly sorry for someone other than myself. But I do now. Only I don't know what to write back to Sister Soledad. An inspiring quote feels too distant, like shouting down a mountain when what Sister S needs is a whisper in her ear. So I close up her letter, unanswered.

There's no mail from Whitney. I'm sure she is mad with me, but I can't scrape up the energy to put together a whole letter, complete with I've-been-so-superhumanly-lame-not-writing-you-back-please-forgive-me apology.

Instead, I find these really dumb Internet jokes and forward them to her, with a little note that says *Funny!* and I feel like a cop-out for doing it, since we both hate that kind of corny stuff.

Finally, I scribble *Write Whitney* on a Post-It, stick it to my screen and hope that does the trick.

My Mother Makes Up
Her Mind About Me

"Do you think we'll ever see him again?"

Mom paces the windows. Back and forth. She could use a widow's walk. Too bad Roy's home improvements never extended to that.

"No," I answer honestly.

"No, not next week? Or no, not ever?"

"No, not . . . for a while." Behind my copy of *Tender Is the Night*, I am crossing my fingers, because I know the truth. No, not ever. Never.

"I wasn't watching him close enough." Pace, pace. "I wasn't paying attention and I didn't see what he needed." Pace, pace. It's making my nerves jangle.

"Roy left," I explain steadily, "because that's his nature. He got bored with suburbia. End of story."

Sometimes too much of the truth is more than Mom needs. I know I've overstepped it, even before I see the shine in the corners of her eyes when she looks over at me. "That sure is a nasty thing to say."

"Well, sorry, but it's not like Roy has this tremendously complicated personality that takes more than fifteen seconds to analyze." Oh, Lordy. Why'd I have to add that? Mom's tears seem to bring out the worst in me.

"You know, Irene, you can be real priggish at times." Mom's voice cracks. "Real priggish."

I lift my book over my face. I might be priggish, but at least I'm not mystified about whether or not dopey Roy is coming back. The guy is probably in some honky-tonk truck stop, watching live televised female mud wrestling, as his one-year-plus-two-months' relationship with Mom turns into memory mildew. Besides, Mom will find someone new. She always does. She's the kind of person who has to live in a pair, same as Whitney.

In *Tender Is the Night*, Dick and Nicole Diver's love wraps around each other so cobra tight that they sign their letters *Dicole*. I wish I could be somebody's *Direne*. A perfect somebody, with the cuteness of Paul Pelicano, the laid-back style of Dan Prior, and a touch of Mr. Rochester's haunted past. He would be named Lars and he would live in Malibu Beach, and when I had to attend glamorous Hollywood events, Lars and I would arrive fashionably late in his steel blue convertible as onlookers murmured *There will never be a love as great as theirs* while snapping our picture from flattering angles.

Mom is still pacing. Poor Mom. I mark my page with Britta's latest postcard and put down my book.

"You want me to walk into town and rent some movies? We could do a whole popcorn-and-movie-night thing."

"Mmm." She stops, drops to the rocker. "Yeah, okay. That might be nice. No horror, though."

But then, just as I'm kicking on my sneakers, Bella phones to invite Mom for a Girls' Night Out.

"Thank God. Now that's *exactly* what I need. Gimme half an hour." Mom hangs up and turns purposeful. I follow her into her bedroom and stand in the doorway, watching as she yanks a comb through her hair and blots on her lipstick.

"So I guess you'll take a rain check on movie night?" I can't help myself from sounding hurt. Mom stops, mid-blot.

"Honey, you know it'd be good for me to get out."

"Why?"

"Because I don't want to sit here and . . . and *dwell* on how I just got dumped."

I clear my throat. "Have you ever noticed how every time a guy dumps you, you dump me?"

"That is not true."

"It is. Because what you really can't stand is being here dwelling on how you're a single mom. You think you're missing out on your real life." I'd heard Mom say something like that once to Marianne, when she hadn't known I was listening. Now I'm slyly glad to throw it at her. "And while we're on the subject of things that are true . . ." But now I have to follow her as she brushes past me in a huff. I talk to the back of her head. "Girls' Night Out is kind of a farce, don't you think? How much about girls could it possibly be, since all you do is go somewhere to check out the guys? What's wrong with Girls' Night In? You could even invite Bella over or—"

"Don't you guilt me, Irene Morse." Mom glares over her shoulder. "There's a box of spaghetti in the cupboard, there's a tomato on the windowsill. I'll be home soon, but don't wait up." She opens the door and slams herself out. Which doesn't surprise me, really, since Mom's first reaction is always to get defensive—a trait I think I got stuck with, too.

The important thing is I said my piece. Whether Mom re-examines it or not will be up to time. I slide back down on the couch and pick up my book. Soon I'm disappearing inside the story, on the coast of Cap d'Antibes, a place that sounds so glitzy and gold-drenched and shimmering that I wish I knew how to pronounce it out loud.

So far, the Dicoles' lives are perfect.

An Unexpected Request

THE RINGING WAKES ME. Mom, too. She must have come home after I fell asleep. I know by the way she's bumping madly down the hall in search of the phone that she is thinking: Roy.

Then she knocks and whispers, "For you!"

When I open my bedroom door, Mom seems more sleepy than angry. Girls' Nights Out are good for her that way, at least. They take the edge off, temporarily. "Tell whoever it is that next time you'll be grounded for any calls past ten, okay?" Then she swoops back into her room.

It takes me a few seconds to realize the phone in my hand means somebody is on the other end. Somebody who wants to talk with me. Now. While I'm still half asleep. "Hello?"

"Irene? It's Drew Fuller."

Drew Fuller? Who is that? "Hi?"

"Is this too late to call?" I can't place his voice, which is soft and gentle, calling to mind guitar players more than football players. "I got your number from an old Bishop Middle snow chain."

"What?" I cough the sleep rasp from my throat. "Are you sure you have the right number?"

"You're Irene, um, Morse?"

"Yes." One thing I'm sure of. "I'm Irene."

"Maybe you don't remember me. I was in Mr. Frank's sixth grade and you were in Mrs. Calderon's fifth, and we were both in the gifted program. We did the Shark Park Project together for science fair?"

The Shark Park Project, how could I forget? It was a proposal petitioning the Fijian government for allocation and protection of a three-mile strip of water off the island of Tonga in order to preserve the near-extinct tiger shark. We were Bishop Middle's official selection, and went on to win fourth place in the State Regionals. I still have the ribbon, although we failed to get the sharks their park.

And now my memory also sifts up a scrawny, silent kid with a mouthful of sharklike silver braces. Why is geeky Drew Fuller calling me at midnight? And am I now supposed to talk to him as if this is a normal, every night occurrence? I give it my best. "Oh, yeah, I remember. Didn't your dad once give some of us rides home?"

"Yep. You still live on Valentine?"

"Uh-huh."

I search for small-talk topics and come up empty-handed. "Why are you calling me?"

"Right. About Tara." Drew Fuller coughs. "Tell Tara Malloy to stop doing that stuff. I saw her steal those candy bars and drinks. You gotta tell her, since you're her friend, that she's crossed the line. Also what she did to my car. My brother and I bought that car together with our own money. You can't believe how mad he was. Tell her enough is enough."

It takes my brain almost a hundred years to process that Drew Fuller from the Shark Park Project is also Starla's beloved, despised D.

He is waiting for me to speak. What should I say first? Should I clarify that she's Starla now, not Tara? Or that I'm not really her friend? Mostly I want to ask Drew Fuller when he got so tall.

Instead, I come up with, "I think *Starla* wants more reasons about why the two of you broke up."

In answer, silence. Then, "We're not each other's types. She's too intense. Can't you tell her that?"

"I'd have a hard enough time explaining that you called me at midnight."

More silence. I can hear the after-echo of my last words, and I wonder if I sounded mean. Then Drew says, in a rush, "Hey, did you know I was Golden Bookworm the year before you? But I only had to read thirty-four books. My class wasn't really into it—otherwise I could have read way more, easy. My kid brother drew vampire bats on my *Bartlett's Quotations*."

"What a brat."

"Nah. It's not like I can't use it." But Drew wouldn't have confessed about the vampire bats unless he thought it was bratty, too. He must love his big, beautiful *Bartlett's* the way I love mine.

"So, you broke my record," he says.

"I guess."

"By, like, seventeen books," he adds.

"Yeah, I guess."

"So . . ." His voice is slightly disbelieving. "How'd you do it?"

"I read plays. That was my librarian's strategy. She was my coach."

"Wanna hear what I read?" he asks, and then starts reeling off his books. As I listen, I can't help but think how strangely exciting it is to be sitting in my bed on a midnight phone call with Drew Fuller. And not metal-mouth, shark-obsessed Drew, but older, better-looking Drew, who is most likely calling me from his house, but who I keep picturing standing behind the register at Shady Shack.

Behind his husky voice, though, I can also hear Starla: *You nerds are all alike. Thinking you're better than anyone else.* What would she say if she knew I was on the phone right now with her very own personal D?

And so when Drew has finished his list, I make myself say, "Okay. And I'll talk to Starla for you tomorrow."

"Wait. Tell me *your* books."

"I can't think of any right now."

"C'mon. Sure you can."

"Well, okay, I read . . . *Monster* and . . . *The Cherry*

Orchard—that's a play. And . . . and . . ." But it's as if somebody is holding a straw to my ear and sucking out my brain through it. There's a roar of emptiness inside my head where my book list should be. "It's so late, I can't think." Then I laugh in a way that sounds suspiciously like a giggle.

Drew laughs, too, as if my impaired conversation is subtly clever.

"I guess I better go," I say. "My mom . . ." But just mentioning my mom makes me feel too self-conscious, and I can't finish.

"Wait," he says again. And then we are both just breathing in and out on the phone. The joined sound of our breath stands up the hair on my arms and the back of my neck. It strikes me that the last thing I would ever want to do is hang up this phone. "I'm almost done with this paperback," Drew says. "It's called *On the Road*. I'll let you have it when I'm through."

"Great." I don't want to tell him that I've already read it. "And I'll . . . I'll talk to Starla tomorrow." I wince. Saying Starla's name is worse than saying Mom. It effectively shatters the moment.

"Okay."

"Good night." No, not *good night*. I could have said anything but *good night*. *Good night* means I am ending the call. What is wrong with me?

"Oh. G'night."

I listen to Drew click off. The hand that held the phone is

damp. I lie down in my bed, my eyes wide on the ceiling. My mind is all noodly and my whole body is tingling. I don't know what to think first. As confusing, as complicated as it is, for the first time this summer, I realize that I am not living in the corner of my life. Something Epic is actually happening to me. Right now. And I didn't even have to move to Los Angeles.

I Attempt to Explain Myself

AN HOUR LATER, I am still awake. I go online. There's one e-mail, from Whitney.

From: wlamott@starpointtenniscamp.org

Um, Irene . . .

Did you send me those bad jokes as a joke? B/c I did not laugh at any. I'll give ya a tax free charity laugh to the one about what do bald guys put for hair color on their driver's license. The others were excroosh. Way thumbs down.

Get this today I find out behind my back Walt told this kid Rich Curie that I looked like an Australian prairie vole. I found one online and it is so so not true but I wonder how many people Rich told. So I broke up with Walt and I'm not speaking to Rich. I will never look at another example of the defect male species. From now on it's tennis tennis tennis and nothing else which is what I should've been concentrating on in the first place . . .

Send me a real letter and no nyuck-nyucks.

W.

Dear Whit——

There's this guy who might like me.

Delete.

Dear Whit——
Do you remember Drew Fuller from a grade ahead of us? Well now he is hot and he called me at midnight.

Delete.

Whitty——
That sucks about Walt. Think of it this way——if you'd married him, you'd be Walt and Whitney Waterman, which sounds like a cartoon and people would be smirky behind your back about it. If you're feeling the need for revenge, you could always start a rumor that he told you he peed his bed until he was twelve.

So there's this guy, but I'm not writing about him right now because I don't want to jinx it. You'll be the first to know if anything happens.

It's almost three in the morning so I'll send a longer letter when I'm conscious.

Your-reen.

Not great, and too brief for what I owe Whitney. But it's better than no mail at all.

It even feels like a jinx to mention Drew at all, but I hit Send.

My Resolution, and Its Sequel

THE NEXT DAY, as soon as I see her, I tell Starla about Drew's call.

I've resolved to tell her because:

A. It is the Heroine thing to do.

B. I would be scared if she found out about the call some other way.

Only Starla gets so angry about it that she can hardly speak, or even look at me. So angry that I wonder if she might take out her key and grate up the paint on Judith's bike. So angry that it makes me angry.

"I didn't do anything," I protest for the second time. "And I especially didn't do anything wrong."

"You never told me you knew him. You lied, basically."

"Because I didn't recognize him. He looked different in sixth grade."

"Whatever."

"You make it seem like Drew calling me is my own fault."

Starla pushes up her bucket hat to scan me from head to foot. Then she rolls her eyes.

"You know, you shouldn't roll your eyes at a person. It's the most critically negative of all facial expressions."

"Then take the hint and go away."

So I keep away from her. I rally the kids for cannonball contests on the dock. We twirl on the raft. We play Marco Polo and Freeze Tag with Zaps and Annie Waldron, who is, as Lainie testified, icky for no real reason. At lunch, I indulge Lainie in three monstrously dull rounds of Twenty Questions. I am the best babysitter of all time, and the self-appointed guardian of all Larkin's Pond kids, because I figure if any of them started drowning, Starla'd be too hostile to perform rescues.

Occasionally, I sneak looks at her. She sits like a bronze-cast, stone-faced goddess on her lifeguard chair. Once she catches my eye, and I half smile over in hopeful truce, but she jerks her head away like I'm some pesky bug not worth more than a second's irritated notice. Underneath, though, I know that each of our minds is fixated on the other, turning obsessive, mental loops.

That afternoon, as I'm packing up, Drew appears.

I try to concentrate on Starla's anger, but Drew dissolves it. I feel the same as I did last night, helplessly, cringingly self-conscious, trying to prepare myself for the aftershock of whatever dumb thing I might say or do in his presence. Odd, nervous thoughts blow in on a gale. *Does my hair look limp and unlustrous? Is my nose still peeling? Has Drew spied the gross bruise halfway up my right thigh?*

"Hi." I smile at him, hoping that I've exposed the correct number of teeth.

"Hey."

"You work in Shady Shack," says Lainie.

"Yeah. Come in next time, and I'll give you a Superblo bubble gum," Drew tells her.

"And me," says Evan.

"Sure." Drew smiles at me over Lainie's head. Didn't he used to wear glasses? I'm pretty sure he did, or how else could I have not noticed those eyes? "You're their babysitter for the summer?"

"Yeah." Starla is watching us too hard for me to relax into the conversation. I get a sense of invisible knives whistling through the air.

"What a cushy job," says Drew. "Babysitting's the easy life, right?"

Cushy? Easy? Most of the time, what I feel about this job is bitter and resentful. Then I'm struck by the possibility that Drew might be having an even worse summer than I am. I look at him harder. Outside and up close, Drew doesn't seem quite as rubber-band bodied as when he's slumped behind a register. His smile is awkward but real.

"Irene loves babysitting us," Lainie declares. "She says we're the best kids she ever took care of."

"I believe it." Drew nods.

"She just takes care of Lainie," Evan adds. "I don't need her."

There's something funny about both kids trying to show off for Drew. I picture him in their estimation, an older guy, as tall as their dad, with his own job and car.

"Hey!" Starla's voice, lilting and sweet, snaps everyone's head around. She is beckoning Drew over.

"The lifeguard wants you," says Evan, his voice loaded with meaning.

"Right, okay," Drew half twists in Starla's direction. "Talk to ya later."

"Bye." I want to say more, only not under Starla's inspection. I open my book and allow myself only the smallest, slyest glances at the two of them. Whatever they're talking about, I console myself that it doesn't seem intimate, though at one point Starla laughs, a pealing bell of a laugh that I'm sure is at least halfway for my benefit. Still, it feels like hours have dragged past before Drew detaches, heading back to Shady Shack, with a quick chin lift to acknowledge us as he passes by.

"So was that guy your boyfriend or something?" asks Evan later, as we're pedaling home.

"No."

"Maybe he wants to be," says Lainie.

"Did he used to go out with the lifeguard?"

"You mean your girlfriend?" I tease.

"Shut up, Irene, she's not my girlfriend," says Evan. "And she's outrageous. If he for-real went out with the lifeguard, there's probably no chance that he likes you."

It's the truth, but it still hits like a sledgehammer.

"Irene would be the number-one girlfriend of anyone, because she makes up so many fun games," says Lainie with such absolute confidence, I could have jumped off my bike and hugged her.

"I'd take hotness over games," Evan answers, equally sincere.

"You're a teenager and Starla is a teenager," muses Lainie, "and that guy from Shady Shack is a teenager, too."

"Yep."

"I can't wait to be a teenager," Lainie bursts out in a fit of passion.

"I'll be thirteen in one year, nineteen weeks, and two days," says Evan. "But you won't be a teenager for a long, long time, crybaby Lainie."

Lainie presses her lips together in a colossal effort not to weep from the unfairness of it all. It makes me feel sorry for her, especially since I remember the Teenager Countdown like it was yesterday.

"C'mon, Lainie," I say. "Race ya to the stop sign."

Intrigue

THAT AFTERNOON, I ask Judith to let me off in town at Organic Fields.

"You sure you want to walk home from here?" she asks. "It's kind of a trek. Longer than from the library."

"It's no problem. I've done it a thousand times," I lie.

"I'll wait in the parking lot and take you home if you want," she persists. "Door-to-door service. Can't beat that."

But I shake my head. I'm already embarrassed that Judith is dropping me here, since I'm sure it will open up another Prior family debate about how Roy's departure has caused Mom to unravel to the heartbreaking point where I'm now in charge of feeding us.

Because Mom isn't unraveling. She's just sad. That's why I want to make her a special dinner.

At Organic Fields, I get half a pound of Gruyère cheese plus fresh bakery bread for gourmet grilled cheese sandwiches. I poke around for the greenest, firmest bunch of asparagus, and I ask for a close-up on three different apple tarts, Mom's favorite dessert. This is a noble gesture on my part since I am more of a chocolate person. I pay with my Food

Chicken money. Guilt money, as I've come to think of it. Best to spend it on a good cause.

At home, I set the table with the blue willow plates that we rarely use, and I write out two little menus, using my calligraphy kit to make the presentation look more restaurant-ish. Then I yank up a healthy bunch of dandelions growing outside by the stoop and I set them in a pewter beer stein. It doesn't look too elegant, but "A weed is a plant whose virtues have not been discovered," I remind myself with one of my favorite Bartlett's.

The phone rings just as I'm forklifting the asparagus out of the steamer.

"Bella and Marianne and some of the other girls all want to do a ladies' poker night." Mom's voice is more cheerful than I've heard in days. "So I'm gonna tag along with them. Can you handle your own dinner?"

I look at the table. "I was going to make us special grilled cheeses. And I bought an apple tart."

"Oh, honey." Then, silence. She wants me to let her off the hook.

"I guess you can have the tart for breakfast, though."

Her relief is audible in her exhale. "That sounds great. And we might go to Smokes after. I'll be late, so please don't call the police to find out about road accidents."

"I won't."

"And put yourself to bed at a reasonable hour. Hey, and honey?"

"Yeah?"

"Thanks for thinking of me, okay?"

"Sure." After I hang up, I skip the grilled cheese and eat an all-asparagus dinner as I read my book. Even inside her insane asylum madness, Nicole Diver's beautiful hair makes my fingers itch. Where-where-where is that notebook? It has to be in my room.

Has to be.

I jump up from the table, full of renewed searching vigor.

In my room, I paw though boxes, toss things from my closet, yank the folders out of my hanging file. I look in ridiculous places, too—my Paul Pelicano envelope and in my underwear drawer and behind my shoe tree. Every second that I can't find it, it's harder for me to stay calm.

When I'm all out of places, I stand there in the middle of my ransacked room, my hands gripping my head, my face and armpits sweaty and angry.

Then a sudden, prickly apprehension hits me with such force that I can't move.

Somebody is outside.

My feet are glued to my rug. Without moving my head, I switch my gaze to my window, into the purplish twilight darkness that soon will be black. Now I can just make out the yew hedge that divides our house from the Binkley property. I stare, paralyzed and unblinking. My eyes adjust to pick out the boxy edge of the Binkleys' station wagon and their rooster weather vane with the broken-off rooster beak.

There, a car is parked out at the edge of our lawn.

Slowly, I sink to all fours and crawl, inch by inch, to the wall light switch. I reach up and snap off my bedroom light. In the dark, I squat on my haunches. My nose itches but I don't dare to scratch. There's no sound except for the steady chirrup of crickets.

Then, from the kitchen door, a knock. My heart leaps. But burglars wouldn't knock first, would they? In a plunge of reckless bravery, I race to the kitchen, and through the window I see the shadowy outline of Drew Fuller. He is standing on the steps outside the kitchen door. He knocks again. I duck again. Oh my God. How can I let him see me like this, so damp and flustered?

"One second!" I yell. Quickly, I scurry to the bathroom, where I click on Mom's makeup mirror. I splash cold water on my cheeks, then find a tube of crusty mascara and apply a coat. I work some Vaseline over my lips, and I fluff out my hopelessly non-heroine hair.

Then I stroll to the kitchen door, breezily snapping on lights. When he sees me through the window, Drew smiles and mouths, "Hi."

I open the door. "Hey, what's up?"

He holds up a copy of *On the Road*. "You'll blast through this," he says. "One of those 'seize the day' kinda books? Makes you feel like you can do anything. Me, anyway." He's wearing faded jeans and a white T-shirt. His tan looks extra dark, his hair extra shiny in the kitchen light. I hope my blasé expression is working as I take the book.

"Thanks."

"Since I was driving through the neighborhood already and the book was already in the car, I thought I'd see if I remembered where you live, and then, if I passed the test and got the house right, I'd say hey and give it to you. To keep. Actually, I've got to go pick up my brother Jake at work. He's older, we share the car so that I'm Tuesday and Thursday, he's the other days, and I only have a junior license anyhow, so he gets to drive more, and I'm kinda running late as it is." Drew is speaking fast and slightly out of breath. "It was an impulse thing," he finishes.

"Oh." I step aside to let him in. "Do you want anything? Like, water or—I have apple tart. Gourmet." I regret the offer immediately, it seems desperate, like I'm trying to seduce Drew Fuller with my private stash of high-end food.

"No, thanks. Jake's not so chill about waiting." Drew frowns as he stares at me. "There's all these black crumbs on your eyelashes."

"Oh, that." My cheeks re-blush. "My mom was trying out makeup products on me. She owns a beauty parlor."

"I know," says Drew. "I remember back when you were in fifth grade, you got your mom to put red stripes in your hair for Halloween. In the library, girls kept coming up to you, asking about it."

I'd forgotten that. "I was Raggedy Ann."

"Uh-huh. It looked wild," says Drew. "Good wild, I mean." There is something about the way he is staring at me that makes me feel as if he'd stared at me back then, too. I imagine myself, lovely and oblivious, sitting at one of the round, blonde-wood library tables, dragging a hand through my red streaky hair as Drew watched me from afar in a quiet agony of longing.

He shifts from foot to foot. "So . . . ," he says.

"So."

"Yeah, it's a good book."

"Oh, right. Thanks . . ."

My voice stops as Drew's fingers reach up suddenly and brush against the outer corner of my eye. I am so startled, I go still. All I feel are his fingertips, friendly, warm, slightly callused. In the back of my head, I hear Starla. *When you let someone do things to you, and he has all this information . . .* But in the thrill of the moment, I push the voice away as Drew drops his fingers to hold my shoulder, his other hand cupping my chin as he lifts it, and in a movement as clear and graceful as anything I've read in any Epic romance, but ten times better because it's happening for real, in my real, true life, Drew leans down and kisses me. His lips meet mine and push, his mouth is open, dry, and when my own mouth opens in half-surprise, half-response, his front teeth click against mine. The reverberation spirals up inside my head and changes everything.

Then we're just staring at each other, and through my surprise I wonder if that was such a good idea. Isn't there supposed to be more that happens before the kiss–like going to a party or the movies, or at least one deep and meaningful conversation about Life, just so that you know you've got a couple of important things in common?

Unless Drew kissed me to get back at Starla. Oh, no. Maybe I'm just a rebound kiss.

"Why'd you do that?" The question is a toad jumping out of my mouth. Starla would never have made such a mood-kill comment.

"Sorry," Drew answers. "I dunno. I better get going," He looks shy.

"I didn't mind," I say quickly.

"Okay." Now he looks mortified. "See you tomorrow?"

"I guess."

Drew pushes open the door, then turns back. "Another impulse thing, I guess. Okay?"

"Sure." He must read something that's better than okay on my face. When he smiles, his eyes twinkle like green glass, as he lets himself out and shuts the door behind. I listen to his feet drumming down the steps, then crunching the gravel. Then I listen to his car drive off. After a few minutes, I open the door and breathe in the warm summer air, which for once doesn't feel too close and steamy, but fragrant and delicious.

Then I run back to the bathroom to examine myself in the

mirror, to see if the imprint of Drew's kiss has made me look any different.

The Irene who looks back at me is definitely someone new, the object of somebody else's fascination. I picture myself in my Halloween streaks, and I shake my head from side to side, letting the ends of my hair brush back and forth against my collarbone. I add some more Vaseline to my lips, smooth my eyebrows, and I tip my face up to an invisible Drew, reliving his kiss in slow motion. The longer I look, the more the image of my reflected self seems secretly tantalizing. Even if Drew had called it an impulse thing, he must have planned it just a little bit. Maybe he'd even been wanting to kiss me since I was in fifth grade, before a kiss from Drew Fuller was even a thought in my head.

Well. I am thinking about it now.

Preoccupations, New and Old

THE DEAFENING ORCHESTRAL *Soundtrack of My Life* makes sleep impossible. After more than an hour of flipping around and kicking at my sheet, I get out of bed and log on to Starla's journal.

STARLAMALLOY'S JOURNAL

Today I Learned that my Witness is a Traiter.
My Witness has been Holding Secret Meetings with
D, where they Talk Secretly and Make Plans.
Witness, if you are Reading this, I Spit on You.
Once Betrayed
This Heart You Frayed
Betrayed Twice
This Heart You Slice

If a bad poem makes you feel rotten, does that mean that on some level, it's good?

For the hundredth time, I reach for Drew's copy of *On the*

Road, which I'd placed on my bedside table. I flip through its soft pages, then bring it to my nose and sniff. I spread my fingers over the pulpy paper, imagining Drew's sun-browned hands on my shoulder again. The book makes me jittery, as if Drew himself is standing in my bedroom.

Sister's e-mail is dull. Little scrips and scraps of her day. She goes on too much about the weather and politics. I can read between the lines that she is sad about Sister Maria Martinez. She doesn't even ask how I am enjoying *Tender Is the Night.* Not that I have been able to concentrate on a single word of the story since Drew left.

I move on to Whitney.

From: wlamott@starpointtenniscamp.org

Attention Delinquent!

This means you Irene Morse! Guess what? Five sentences do not make a letter. Can I remind you that you pulled this same silent treatment trick on me last summer when my parents took me to England for three weeks? Let me refresh your memory. First you made a big dumb point of reading like nine thousand books by British authors so that you knew thirty thousand things about the U.K.—just to show that the less-deserving person was the one who got the plane ticket. Then from the day I left it was nothing but radio silence from the USA. In the beginning I figured Dad's international cell was just one of his dud "I-got-a-deal-on-a" deals. Next I decided my e-mails must be collapsing on a giant technical glitch midway across the ocean. Finally I decided (hoped!) you were going back to ye olde days of paper and doodles like those notes we passed in Phonics and I got all repsyched thinking about the four or five via airmailed letters I'd be getting all at once.

Instead I got—nada. And to refresh your memory when I came home your lame excuse was that you had a cold. So if you don't write me with one real thing really happening in your life we're going to have some serious friendship issues when I get back and yes you can take that as a threat.

While I'm on the subject of England I better tell you about this Guy here (a guy named Guy I'm so un-kidding it's a completely real name in England where he's from) who's been giving us all the best slang. Like winge means to whine and a posh toff is a rich snob and someone who is scaly is a creep and hectic means out-of-control. Guy whispers me naughty bits of U.K. vocab in private and in that saucy 007 accent I am putty in his hands.

Just goes to show—you don't have to go to England to find yourself a scrumptious crumpet, luv!

So stop giving me the silent winge just cuz you think I'm having a toff summer. I mean it Irene. No fair to act so scaly to the same person who made you homemade protein sorbet when you had laryngitis or who stood in line for three hours to snag you those words beyond boring *Poetry Speaks* tickets so you could have a posh birthday. I want life details.

xo anyway,
Whittle

This time, I don't even have to think before I start typing.

Dear Whit——

You are right. I don't have a cold. I don't have any excuse. Except——have you ever liked a guy so much that just thinking about him is like somebody pouring ice water down your spine? Have you ever stood next to a guy whose simple fact of existence was enough to make your insides do backflips?

The guy is Drew. He is almost six feet tall and has silvery green eyes and he has a lowish softish voice that reminds me of smoke, and his smile makes me die. I don't know where things are right now with us, it's so new even writing about it makes me feel like I might break the spell.

I'm sorry I haven't given you more life details but as you can see, I've been kind of preoccupied.

Also, I want you to know that the *Poetry Speaks* tickets were the best birthday present I ever got in my life.

Is this letter real enough?

xo back from

Me

I Am Given a Reprieve

MAYBE IT'S THE book's cover—the bend of road and inky blue sky leading the eye up and away—but the next morning when I see Drew's *On the Road*, I decide to tuck my own, worn, identical copy inside an envelope and send it to Sister Soledad, with a note about seizing the day.

Drew's copy I'll keep forever.

I place the package in the mailbox and pull up the flag. I'm sure that Sister's already read it, but maybe the surprise mail will cheer her up.

Mom is still sleeping off her girls' poker night, which turned out to be another late one, so I eat a banana on the stoop as I wait for Judith. It's going to be another beautiful summer day, which depresses me because I don't particularly want to go to Larkin's and see Starla, even if it also means seeing Drew. I'd rather see Drew on non-Starla territory, and her sad-angry poem of betrayal jounces in my head. What if she can tell just by the look on my face what happened to me last night?

Lucky for me, the Prior kids have a fresh distraction.

"We got a fridger-fraidy box!" screeches Lainie the second

I'm out of the car. She points to the enormous cardboard box on the front lawn, just in case I might have missed it. "Dad brought it home from work last night. His office got a new fridger-fraidy and he says we can do anything we want with it. Will you help us do something, Irene? Please please please?"

"Sure, as long as I never have to hear you say the word *fridger-fraidy* again."

Judith's mouth opens, but then she just snaps it shut, smiles at us all and waves good-bye.

"It's as big as a closet," says Evan, walking around it. "It could be a lot of things. Mom said we should spend an hour brainstorming ideas."

The brainstorm lasts five minutes. Evan's first brilliant scheme is to cut the refrigerator box open, fill it with cushions, then jump into it from a branch of the backyard elm tree on the slim hope of landing safely inside.

"I don't like those odds," I tell him.

Lainie wants to turn the box into a castle and dig a moat around it.

"Your parents weren't happy about how the lawn looked after Mud Monster," I remind her, "so I'm not sure how well a moat would go down."

"How about a pirate ship?" says Evan.

Lainie pouts. "That's too much of a boy idea."

"Not if you include mermaids and treasure chests," I coax.

Miraculously, Lainie comes around. We draw up a plan to seal the box with duct tape, and then cut a square trapdoor as the only entrance into the body of the pirate ship. Evan wants it to have a mast and sail.

"All I need is two wrapping-paper tubes." Evan dashes to the house and reappears a minute later. "See, then I can attach these vertically and cut a hole right here to stabilize the tube, and I'll knot a bed sheet to the top," he says. "Think Mom'll let me use one of the spare sheets?"

"Go for it," I tell him, and he races to the house again.

Lainie looks to me for our grand counter-plan.

"I'm warming up by drawing portholes," I say.

"That's boring."

"Skulls and crossbones?"

She smiles and skips off in search of her glow-in-the-dark crayons.

By noon, it's broiling, but the kids are too deep into the project to quit. I use a paper plate to trace some portholes, and then draw a treasure chest for Lainie to color. Later, I go inside and slap together cheese sandwiches, which I bring outside along with a jug of orange juice.

"Hey, let's eat lunch in the ship's galley!" Evan yells.

"Too hot." I sit on the lawn. The pirate project has become tedious. I would much rather be at Larkin's. It's unsettling to think of Drew and Starla there together, but it's worse being sidelined out here, drawing skulls and missing out.

Lainie's head pops out of the trapdoor to badger me again. "Come in here with us!"

"Not now." I lie down on my back, peel the crust off my

sandwich and speculate on what Drew is doing right now. I feel his kiss, his kiss, his kiss again. My brain rewinds and plays it out over and over. I think about how people change, how Gifted Program Drew Fuller, who evolved into Starla's D, might now turn out to be my Drew, maybe.

Thoughts of Starla distract me, too. Has Drew talked with her today? Does he think she looks better in her red bathing suit or her yellow one? Does he think she's the most gorgeous girl he ever met, and if not, why not? Will Drew ask Starla if she knows where I am today? What if they're talking about me right now? Or what if, after kissing me, Drew has decided I fail miserably as a kisser, and he wants Starla back? My body flinches to imagine it.

A shadow falls over the grass. I look up. Knuckles to hips, Lainie stares down. "You aren't being excited enough about our pirate ship."

I pop the rest of my sandwich in my mouth and brush my hands together. "Okay. I've only worked on this thing all day. What do you command me to do now?"

"Come on, Irene, don't joke," she whines. "Be how you normally are. Make us paper pirate hats, or tell us some scary pirate stories."

Evan, who is eavesdropping, ducks his head shyly back inside the box, so I presume he agrees.

"I'm taking a break right now."

"Your break's been long enough. Besides, you promised to

draw me a mermaid. How about we make the kind that sticks out from the front of a ship?"

"Nooo . . . ," Evan moans from in the box.

"Maybe later," I say.

"Maybe never!" booms Evan.

"Shut your big fat trap, Evan!" screeches Lainie, whirling all of her anger onto him. "A pirate ship *is* more about boys, anyhow! I should get at least one mermaid for my good collopilation!"

"Be quiet, baby! We hate it when you talk in baby talk, don't we, Irene?"

Lainie runs over to the box and kicks it. The box jerks as Evan punches back.

"Ha ha, you didn't hurt me!" Lainie kicks the box again.

"Cut it out, you two." And then I realize I'm truly fed up. After all, it's not my duty to sit out here all afternoon in this bone-melting heat, breaking up fights until these kids get bored with their refrigerator box pirate ship. I have plenty of other things on my mind these days, way more stimulating things than drawing portholes and mermaids. Besides, what part of my meager babysitting contract requires that I have to provide nonstop entertainment for Evan and Lainie Prior? Not to mention that they've seriously damaged my future desire for children of my own. How will I ever think of the word *baby* without the word *sitter* caught in its sticky grip?

"I'm going in," I say. "I want to watch my soap opera."

"What soap opera?" Lainie blinks back the tears in her eyes.

"Let her go," mumbles Evan. "She's a grouch today. Probably got her period."

"Ew," says Lainie, and she looks at me in faint horror.

"Whatever chance you had of my staying out here," I say to Evan, "you just lost with that adorable little comment."

"Except *I* didn't say anything bad!" Lainie wails. "Come back, Irene! Please! Come back to me!"

But I've had it, and I walk inside and slam the front door behind me.

When I look out the window, the kids are out of view, having dragged the refrigerator box off to somewhere in the backyard. Eventually, I hear them squealing together in obnoxious sibling unity.

I click to Whitney's favorite soap opera. Even though I only watch it when I'm over at Whitney's house, I'm fully up to speed on the plot by the next commercial break. That's the nice thing about soap operas. A hundred things happen and nothing changes. A man and woman share a deep onscreen kiss, and I watch their technique with more interest than usual. I stretch the recliner to its laziest adjustment. A pleasant heaviness itches inside my eyelids.

A nap would be so good right now . . .

The sound of the car pulling into the drive makes me bolt awake, blinking. How long have I been dozing? A new soap opera has replaced Whitney's. Outside, I hear the brake pull and the engine cut.

Great. Of all days for Judith or Dan to come home early, of course it would have to be the one time when I'm shirking.

But when I look out the window, it's not a purple jelly bean or a dusty pickup I see. It's Drew's car. And Starla and Drew are climbing out of it.

Visitors

"WHAT'S UP?" Starla smiles as I open the front door. She is wearing an ice-blue tube top with a miniskirt so small, I could fold it up into my shorts pocket. But it's Drew, trailing behind, who has the self-conscious look on his face. "I asked him if he could give me a ride to where you worked," Starla explains, jabbing her thumb over her shoulder. " 'Cause I'd been thinking to myself, 'Hey, I haven't seen my nerd buddy in almost a week.' So he said he'd drop me off."

Drew looks like he can't quite figure out how he's managed to create such an awkward situation. His eyes hold mine. Has he been thinking about The Kiss as much as I have? I can't tell by his face how strong our connection of last night holds up to the light of today.

Meanwhile, mischief has lit up Starla's face like a candle as she trots inside.

Lainie, Evan, and Poundcake have trooped in to stand behind me.

"Hi!" says Starla in her most sugary voice.

"Hi." Lainie looks at me. "We better double check with

Mom about having guests," she stage-whispers. "Do you want me to call her?"

"No. They only stopped by for a couple of minutes," I say. My voice sounds unnaturally stern. "Go back outside and play."

"I don't have to go back anywhere," says Lainie. "This is my house."

"Come on, Lainie," says Evan. "We've got some secret stuff to finish up outside, anyhow."

"Oh, right." Lainie wriggles her eyebrows. "Top secret. Meaning, we're not telling *you*, Irene." She sticks out her tongue, but they both leave, dragging the dog behind.

"Cute kids," says Starla. "That boy made me feel his biceps the other day." She makes a motion of pinching something indescribably tiny, and her laugh is mean, and I feel sorry for Evan. "So are you gonna be a good hostess and offer us anything to drink?" Starla moves past me, looking for the kitchen, but turns in the direction of the living room. I follow her. "Wow, this place is a snore. No pool. No neighbors. What do you do all day, anyhow? It's not like you can drive."

"We have bikes," I say.

"Except the only place you can go is Larkin's," says Starla. "Funsie fun." I figure that she came by to embarrass me on purpose, to prove how superior she is to me in every way. I look back over at Drew, who has stopped in the front hall, in front of the bookshelves.

"Boring but relaxing, I bet," he says to me, and smiles.

I nod. "Sometimes I like hanging out here better than Larkin's."

"Are you kidding? I'd go insane here," says Starla.

"Larkin's was packed today. Now *that* was a mob to drive you insane." Drew's hands are pouched so deep in his cargo shorts' pockets, they look as though they'd split the seams. Starla laps the living room and dining room before doubling back.

At the kitchen door, Poundcake is howling and scratching to be let in. Loud as that is, I can also hear Evan teasing Lainie, and Lainie screeching at Evan. What would Judith or Dan think if they pulled up to this chaos?

"There's nothing to drink," I say, brisk, brisk, brisk, "and this family's crazy health nuts, so unless you want some alfalfa sprouts for the road, there's nothing to eat, either. Maybe I'll see you guys later?"

"Chill out," says Starla. She puts a hand on the banister. "What's upstairs, anyhow?"

"Nothing," I answer. "Rooms."

"Mmm." Now she strolls into the kitchen, where she opens the refrigerator door. I follow her and Drew follows us absently, his nose stuck in one of Dan's travel books.

"Orange juice. Skim milk." Starla looks baffled. "Where's the real drinks?"

"I told you, they don't have that kind of stuff. But listen, they'll be home soon, and if you're still here, that won't look good for me. You two should take off." I look to Drew. "Okay?"

He glances up from the book, which he is trying to disappear inside. I know that trick. "Yeah, sure."

"In a minute." Starla takes three glasses from the cupboard and fills each with water from the tap. "Water?" She hands a glass to Drew.

He takes the glass and sits at the kitchen table, flipping through the book. Where was the guy from last night, whose hand on my shoulder was so sure? There's been a downshift in Drew's personality. I'm impatient that he won't speak up or make a decision.

I deliberately pour out the water from my glass and balance it in the drying rack. "All I mean is you could get me into real trouble."

"What's the harm of visiting?" Starla bumps around the kitchen. She centers a magnet over the school snapshot of Lainie on the fridge, then pockets a penny from the glass change jar on the windowsill. At last she slouches into a kitchen chair, her tanned legs stretching out endlessly from her inch of miniskirt, and she stares at Drew until he stops reading.

"This is a good book," he says. "I always wanted to see the Galápagos. The finches and Darwin and everything." He looks over at me, and I am certain I feel a flash of last night in the perk of his interest, in the focus of his eyes right on me. "Have you been anywhere cool?"

"Canada," I say. That's my standard lie. I haven't been anywhere at all, but Canada always seems reasonable.

"He didn't ask me one question on the whole drive over," Starla says, dropping her head back to yawn at the ceiling. "I was asking everything about his day, right? He says fine and fine and hardly anything else."

"We could talk about what you did to my car," says Drew. "We could talk about how you've been some kind of freak to me ever since the end of school."

"Since we broke up, you mean."

Drew shrugs. "Okay. Since then."

"If I'm so psycho, why'd you drive me here the second I asked you?"

"Maybe I'm trying to keep things normal, since I never know what you're gonna do next."

"Or you wanted an excuse to come over."

Drew doesn't speak for a moment. I realize I'm holding my breath. "So what?" he says. "What do you care why I do what I do?"

Starla's eyes ping-pong from me to Drew and back to me, trying to figure everything out about us. "I've got an idea," she says, drawing out the words slowly. "Let's play Truth or Dare."

"Truth or Dare? But that's a kid game." Last time I played Truth or Dare was at Britta's eleventh birthday party, where my dare—for Ali Magros to wear a pair of her older brother's briefs over her jeans while singing "Baa Baa Black Sheep" on the front porch—was considered the top dare of the night.

"Only if you play it like a kid." Starla gives me her standard look of bored contempt. "Go, give me a dare. A serious dare."

Now I'm confused. What does *serious* mean? Do I dare Starla to do something that would put her in danger, like shove a Cheerio all the way up her nose or hold her finger over an open flame? "I dare you to drink a tablespoon of Tabasco."

"Nerd, get a clue," Starla dismisses me. Then looks to Drew. "You. Do a dare."

Drew doesn't hesitate. "I dare Irene to make out with Tara in the closet for thirty seconds."

Then they both start laughing, and suddenly Drew and Starla both seem a lot older than me. Outside, I hear Lainie and Evan screeching around the house, playing tag. While half of me is rooted motionless to my chair, the other half wishes more than anything that I could run outside and join in their game.

"Arright. You heard him. Let's go." Starla is already out of her seat. She pushes out her lips and makes a kissy sound.

"Are you joking?"

"Of course not. It's a *dare*. Come on." She takes my hand and propels me out to the hallway, where she finds the closet, scoots me in with her and shuts the door.

The inside of the closet smells like mothballs and rubber rain boots. I'm just playing along, I figure. Nobody's forcing me to make out with anybody. Though I can hear my own heartbeat running scared in my ears. Then Starla starts. "Understand one thing, okay? Drew's not your territory," she whispers. I can't see her face, but her words come fast and damp and land like warm dew on my face. "I don't care if he likes you, and I really don't care if you're madly in love with him, since I'm not ready for him to be like that with anyone yet, okay? So on your next turn, you better dare me to make out with him."

"Next turn?" I hiss. "Forget it. There is no next turn. I quit this game."

"Fine. After your dare." The grip of her skinny fingers on my forearms is painful. "Got it?"

"And I'm not madly in—"

"Liar." And then Starla moves closer, filling the dark space between us, and she kisses me, hard, as she opens the door. Starla's kiss is nothing like Drew's kiss. Her mouth is flat and small, and her lips are soft, and she makes an almost joking, smacked-together sound with them, but then there's a little bit of spit on my lower lip from where her mouth has been, and after she's done, I'm too surprised to speak.

We come stumbling out of the closet. "We did it," Starla sings out. She ambles back to the kitchen and slumps back into her chair, swinging her feet up to balance, ankles crossed, on Drew's lap. I feel woozy. Food Chicken dares seem like a million years ago.

"For real?" Drew looks impressed. It occurs to me that he likes this game. "How was it?"

"Okay," I say.

"Was it really thirty seconds?"

"It was over thirty seconds," says Starla, "because she wouldn't stop." At this, Drew looks even more impressed, so I don't speak out in protest. "Now it's your turn," Starla commands me. "Go."

Following her order is the last thing I want to do, but I'm scared. The situation has fallen so far out of my control that I don't want to make it more complicated. I'll just do what Starla says, and hope they leave soon. So, in a small bird voice, I say, "I dare you to kiss Drew."

"Aw, you put her up to that," Drew accuses Starla. But he doesn't sound as concerned as he does amused. It's strange how he keeps shifting shapes before my eyes, one minute the old, boy Drew, the next minute a mysterious guy I feel like I just met.

Starla stands up and walks around the table and stops about a foot in front of Drew. "Everyone says I'm the totally best-looking girl in school," she says, looking over at me. "What do you think?"

"Yes," I say. "You are."

"I could be a model," she says. "I could be an actress."

"You'd make a good actress, that's for sure." Drew snorts. "Everything's a drama with you."

Starla laughs. "Don't be scared," she teases. "It's only a friendship kiss."

"You're the one who didn't want to be friends," says Drew

in a tone so private, I feel like an intruder just by listening. "Jeez, Tara. I tried to be your friend."

"And now I'm trying to be yours," Starla answers.

"Then how about let's call it a good-bye kiss."

She doesn't answer him, and I can tell that Drew's comment was not what Starla was hoping for. And then in that next moment Drew pulls her hand so that Starla drop-slides onto his lap, and her arms fall over his shoulders and her head dips, and he balances his hands lightly on either side of her waist, and right before their mouths meet, I catch Starla's eye, quick as the dart of a minnow, and I know what she is thinking, that I am the Witness, and what is going on here is not completely about Drew anymore. I watch them kiss, and it's sort of awful, except that it's also exciting, seeing an up-close, real-live, long, wet kiss, even if I'm not part of it.

And then from outside there's all this yelling and it takes me a second to realize that the voice belongs to Evan, and that it's my name he's yelling, and that something is wrong.

I Mess Up

WHEN JUDITH ARRIVES at the hospital, she flops into the chair next to mine and puts her hand on top of my hand.

"Breathe easy," she says. "It's only a broken arm. You're white as a sheet, Irene."

"It was my fault," I say. "I wasn't outside, and—"

Judith shakes her head. "Children get into scrapes all the time. They're built to take these kinds of knocks."

But I'm sick to the pit of my stomach. Images of the past hour whoosh back and forth in front of my eyes. Lainie on the ground at the base of the elm tree. Poundcake hacking up yellow bile. Evan hollering in my ear, "I told her I'd test it! I told her I'd jump first!" Starla, quiet, blinking at the refrigerator box full of pillows, her lifeguard skills dried up on land. Drew kneeling next to Lainie, asking where it hurts. Finally, the five of us packing into Drew's car to the hospital.

I've called Mom, and Judith has called Dan, who arrives before Lainie is finally presented, wearing an icing-pink arm cast with sling, and chattering happily about how brave the doctor and nurses told her she was.

Drew and Starla stick around for a while, too, until Starla

asks Drew to take her home. As they leave the waiting room, she pinches his side. "Come on, *buddy*," she says. Drew jumps away from the pinch, but otherwise doesn't act standoffish toward her, and my heart falls as I watch them leave the building and cross the parking lot, Starla bumping her hip against Drew's in that easy, joking way that can only look graceful if a person is built long and willowy. Maybe that good-bye kiss was even better than it looked–and it looked pretty good.

It's crushing to think that Starla and Drew might be getting back together again. But how could I have ever competed with Starla? I was an idiot to think so.

Dan drops me off at my house. Mom is sitting in Granny Morse's chair, flipping magazines and humming along with Roy's blues CD.

"I just got off the phone with Judith," Mom says. "She didn't sound angry with you." In Mom-speak, this means she is taking her cue from Judith and isn't mad, either.

"Yeah, it could have been worse."

I sprawl on the couch, locate my book underneath it and try to read. But the dullness of the evening falls all around me, especially when I contrast it with everything that happened this afternoon. After all that action, I feel ill at ease to be so still.

The deadly quiet must be getting to Mom, too. When Bella calls, Mom flies for her purse and keys. "You don't mind, do you, honey? The girls are all over at McGillicutty's."

I shake my head. "I guess not," I say reluctantly.

"My cell phone's on, I won't be late, and I'll bring home a turkey burger for you, all right?"

"Okay."

After she's gone, I feel an extra surge of restlessness. I pick up the phone to make sure it has a pulse, and I realize that I am hoping to hear from Drew. Fat chance. He and Starla are probably taking some moonlit walk, chuckling together about how a not-even-freshman almost came between their passionate romance, while Starla quotes her own love rhymes. My only consolation is that Drew must realize how bad Starla's poetry is, right down to the flaws in meter.

I roam around the house until I end up sitting on my bed, staring at my bookshelf, although another long night of reading doesn't exactly entice me. I close my eyes and imagine all of the characters from my favorite stories springing from their books, rushing from the shelf into my head like guests to a party. It's something I used to do when I was little, to make myself feel less alone. Then I reach out and touch the spine of my most beautiful book, my *Bartlett's Familiar Quotations*, which is inscribed with my name in gold leaf. That was a great day, even when that kid booed since he thought I had cheated. A truly great day cannot be wrecked by one boo.

Tender Is the Night, which I still haven't finished, is resting on the couch. I decide I'll take it down to the basement, where I know I won't be able to hear the phone, even it does ring, which it won't.

I scoop up the book, then open the door to the basement

and stare down the steps. It's as dark as a ditch, but the temperature is heavenly, and it reminds me of this story I read about a man who climbs down to the bottom of a well, but then somebody takes away his ladder so that he can't get back up, and so he sits and contemplates his life and all the choices he made that led him all the way down to this moment, and then finally he decides that being stuck at the bottom of a well is not such a grave fate, after all.

I hold the raw wood railing hard and take it one step at a time.

A few years ago, Mom had tried to turn the basement into a sewing room. She got Bruno, her boyfriend at that time, to haul an armchair down here, along with a floor lamp, a sewing table and a sewing machine that hasn't been switched on in so long, it probably doesn't even know what it is anymore. My sleeping bag is here, too. I curl up in the chair and pull the sleeping bag around me and practice my contemplating. Too soon, my contemplations turn to sensations, of Drew's hand on my chin, of Starla's breath on my cheek, and then Drew's kiss, then Starla's kiss, then Drew's kiss again, sensations that twist achingly through me, and I wish I had more exciting options in store for tonight than my long, lonely basement exile.

I open my book and take a crack at it, but that doesn't do the trick, either, because in ten seconds I am back to thinking about Drew again.

He's not going to call please let him call. Should I be the one to call him?

Tonight I'd trade any Epic for an eventful chapter of my own life. A dark basement can't offer the same pulse-stopping spark of real-life possibility. I am fidgety and agitated inside myself. I know I'd risk anything–even Drew's rejection–for just one more exhilarating moment of his presence.

The Dicole's lives are falling apart, too, but my problems seem way worse.

Reality Gives Me a Nudge

MOM COMES HOME early and then, too soon, goes to bed, leaving me alone again, and very awake. There's a note from Whitney that came in earlier, which I'd been saving to read until just before I went to bed, like dessert.

From: wlamott@starpointtenniscamp.org

My-rene—your letter shocked me out of my peds! Oh My God it sounds like you've hooked a total Paul Pelicano. Send me more deets on your man as they happen.

Can you believe we're almost to the end of summer? Can you believe that we are almost about to be freshmen? Eeeek! Hey Britta's last postcard she was all on my case for never writing her any postcards but it's like who's not on e-mail? I wouldn't even know how to find stamps! Her and her dad went to visit her aunt in San Somewhere and Brit never hooked up with that Ernesto dude after all. Guess not everyone can have as hot and sweaty a summer as us right?

I come home in less than 2 wks—can't wait to see you soooooon.

xo W.

Hot and sweaty. I wish. And Whitney's reminder that the high school countdown is almost up refreshes my anxiety about it. Am I ready? Would I even know if I am? Either way, thinking about Whitney coming home bursts through me with so much happiness I have to let her know.

Dear Whit,

As much as you are missing me, I'm missing you Doubles——a little tennis humor for ya. As soon as you get home you better call me. I've already bought two cans of chocolate-pudding frosting and a bag of dipping chips which are stashed under my bed, waiting for your return.

I pause, then make myself write:

I'm not sure it's really going on anymore with Drew, so Britta and I'll have to live vicariously through your steamy romance escapades. I never wrote her either——but then who'd want a postcard from exotic New Jersey?

But I've still got lots to report, and I'll fill you in when I see you soon soon soon! xoxo

Reeny

I move on to Starla. She has posted some new pictures, some from her friend Kelli's weekend pool party, and others from a school baseball game. The baseball ones are old pictures, from spring, but it's a shock seeing Drew.

In one photo, Starla is walking along the bleachers a few steps behind Drew, who wears board shorts, a green jacket and a baseball cap. In another, they sit on a plaid blanket; both have on sunglasses and look untouchably cool. Drew's hand is folded over Starla's, and they are looking up as if the photographer has interrupted a private joke. In just these few images, Starla once again has turned me into an uninvited, irrelevant spectator.

Under the plaid blanket picture, Starla has scripted:

Re-United. Hey Witness! More where that came from!

She is bluffing, of course, since the pictures are outdated. More interesting, she feels the need to lie, which might mean she is—what? Warning me? Trying to make me feel suspicious and jealous? How strange that Starla Malloy could see me as even the smallest threat.

But there won't be any more of where that came from for me, because I decide that I am not going onto her blog again. The romance of Starla and Drew is not something I will suffer through. If they're back together as a Drewla, I won't let her postings of their Epic be my consolation prize. And if they're not back together, well, I won't let myself think about that just yet.

I shut down the computer.

A Heroic Twist

THE NEXT DAY, Judith phones and says she's sending the kids to Orlando until the end of August to visit Dan's mother. It was kind of a casual, last-minute thing, Judith explains, after their gran called for an update on Lainie's arm.

"So it all works out in the end, right?"

"Unless you count the part about me being out of a job." Though I don't say this until I've hung up. And I am skeptical about how casual and last-minute this plan really was. Maybe Dan and Judith are more judgmental than they'd let on, and have pegged me as an unfit babysitter.

Mom does not rush to take me back at Style to Go, and when she does concede to put me on the payroll, I'm only there for three days of the week, and with limited duties. On my first free day, I celebrate by going into town to pick up a frozen burritos dinner, a new stack of library books from Miss Kitamura and fresh filters for the air conditioner.

Mom has beaten me home. "Thought we'd finally make it our Girls' Night In," she tells me. "I picked up some movies. Won't this be fun?"

"Yeah, sure. Great." I try to look enthusiastic, though I'm

not entirely convinced a Bella call won't be coming through any minute.

Mom is attempting to master Roy's parting gift, an impossibly reconfigured remote control, and I'm microwaving the burritos when I hear a knock at the kitchen door.

I whirl around and through the window I see Drew. There is no way I can hide my startled reaction. He's wearing a T-shirt printed with the words *Miles Away from Ordinary*. Which is somewhat ironic, since I've spent the past few days trying to convince myself of just how totally ordinary Drew Fuller is, and how I don't care one bit that he and Starla are back together. Convictions that are now leaking out of me into a puddle of confusion, especially since the main thought spinning through my brain is how I wish I hadn't let my hair air-dry into its natural state of a million cowlicks.

But I open the door anyway.

"Hey."

"Hey."

"I came by to ask you how your kid's arm was doing."

"Lainie's okay. She's in Florida. You could have just called." Which I regret saying as soon as I say it.

"You could just give me a break." Drew smiles his at-least-one-mile-away-from-ordinary smile.

I smile back, then move aside. "Come on in."

"Who's that?" Mom sings out merrily from the living room. I lead Drew into the living room for a round of clumsy introductions. "Nice to meet you, Drew. Right on time for movie night," says Mom. "We even have an extra cheese burrito." I cringe. Words like *movie night* and *extra cheese burrito* suddenly, inexplicably mortify me. As soon as I can, I steer Drew back into the kitchen.

"Do you want something to drink?"

"Sure."

I take two canned teas from the fridge and toss Drew one. Drew pops the top and then we just stand there.

"We could go outside for a walk," I suggest.

"Okay."

I lean into the living room doorway. "We're going to take a walk outside."

Mom frowns. "What about our movie?"

"Don't wait, just start without me. I won't be long."

She looks hurt, but she doesn't have a leg to stand on and she knows it.

The sun is setting, turning the edge of the sky tangerine. We walk, close but not touching, to the end of Valentine Way. Drew tells me that he's given his two weeks' notice at Shady Shack, and then we talk about summer ending and school starting, and even though it's small talk, it's not as stilted as it could be, considering that I'm supplying exactly zero from the witty rapport department.

When we sit on the curb, side by side, the space between us feels charged with opportunity, and I still haven't gotten up the nerve to ask Drew what's going on with him and Starla.

"We're not," he says abruptly. I blink.

"Not what?"

"We're not together. Me and Tara. If you were curious."

"No, I wasn't." I shrug. "It's not my business." Then I can't help it. "But then, why–what about the Truth or Dare? Because . . ." I make myself say it. "Because I think you do like her. Or at least partly. And I know she likes you."

"I think I really tried to like her," Drew agrees with a nod. "But most of the time, she confused me, if you want to know the truth. Any guy at school would've killed to spend time with Tara. But in the end, you can't keep going out with a girl just to impress the guys at school. In the end, it was just Tara and me, and we didn't match. Then what she did, after, the stealing and keying my car. She was always acting so dumb." He finishes his iced tea in one long *ulp*ing noise.

"Starla's not dumb." Though I don't know if I'm saying this because I mean it, or because it seems like a gracious-heroine trait to come to the defense of my rival.

"Nah, I didn't mean it that way. Look, Tara's cool. I mean, she knows how to get attention. She's got absolutely everything it takes to make people notice her." Which is true, so I try not to look like Drew's words are stomping all over me. "But once you do notice her, that's it. I was honest with her about it once. I told her I felt like I was doing something wrong, dating her because of her looks."

I shrink inwardly, wondering how Starla must have taken that. "That does seem kind of mean."

"Well, why else would I hang out with her?" Drew asks.

"All she talks about is her friends and the mall, and even when I went on her blog, all that was on it was stuff about the mall and her friends."

"And her poems," I remind him. We exchange a look.

"Yeah, probably I should take the blame for those," says Drew. "I must not be very inspiring."

"You are!" I say, though this comes out a little louder than I'd intended.

"Thanks." Drew looks away, leaning back on his elbows. He pulls up a blade of grass and rolls it in his mouth. I glimpse his stomach, a smooth brown line.

"But, hey, I don't want to hang out all night talking about Tara." He looks at me sidelong, and my insides liquefy. "That's not the reason I came over."

And then Drew and I finally have the conversation that I'd wished had come before The Kiss. We talk about school, and parents, and music, and tennis camp, and Canada (I have to improvise on this topic), and the Galápagos, and who was Bartlett, anyway?, and favorite foods, and grossest foods, and God. Our topics run all over the place, and at some point in the middle of all that talking, Drew kisses me again. At first every muscle of my body is tense that my neighbor Mrs. Binkley is Humbert-ishly watching us, but then I melt into it, I can't help myself, since it's just as good as the first one—better, actually.

It's not an impulse thing, either. Kissing Drew this time is deliberate, it feels like a message, maybe a promise of something that is beginning. Even when he resumes talking about whether he'll take soccer or football for fall sports and how his brother is going away to college, my breathless inner voice can't stop chattering, *Drew Fuller wants to see me again. Drew Fuller wants to kiss me again.*

The shadows of dusk bring out hollows in Drew's face, and watching him, suddenly I see a more mature Drew, and it scares me a little bit. I think about all my countdowns, how they have lifted me up to this hour of perfection that feels so fleeting, I almost wish it wasn't happening at all. Here I am, feeling Drew's arm closing up the space between us to brush against mine, listening to his voice falling and rising, hearing the distant chime of an ice cream truck, wincing at a sharp piece of gravel that bites into the back of my thigh as I adjust position—here I am inside the thousand separate sensations that make up this single, counted-down moment, and I'm totally exhilarated, but I can't make it stay.

Drew has been talking about how jealous he is that his brother is going to school in California.

"My friend Whitney and I call it L.A.N.J.," I tell him.

"What's that?"

"Life After New Jersey. When you start to have options."

Drew laughs hard, which gives him a short hiccup attack. It's vintage Shark Park behavior, except that it's not, since the Drew of today isn't the same Drew anymore. His non-braces smile that broke Starla's heart has stolen mine, too, I guess, but in a way, I also have some information, the information of the old Drew underneath the new Drew. It feels like an advantage.

Maybe Starla is right. Maybe nerds do like to stick together.

Drew walks me home. We linger at his car, and we discuss going to see a movie the next night. My buzz lasts in the minutes after he's driven away. Through the living room window, I see the back of Mom's head peeking over the couch. She's just started the second movie.

"Okay, give me the rundown. Is that your boyfriend?" she asks. But she doesn't shape the question in a teasing way, and I am grateful enough for that to answer sincerely.

"Not yet."

"He's cute."

"Yeah?"

"Oh, yeah. I thought you'd be gone even longer."

"Well, I didn't want to miss our Girls' Night In."

"That's sweet of you. But we could have done Girls' Night In tomorrow night."

"Actually, I'm going out with Drew tomorrow night."

"Really?"

"So I guess we should grab our Girls' Nights In while we can."

And if she gets my point, Mom doesn't act defensive. Instead, as I slide next to her, she flops an arm around me so that we are both stretched out, toe-to-toe and equally balanced on the couch.

Affirmed and Resolute

From: Soledad@olothtrc.com

Dear Irene,

When I received *On the Road,* I knew what you were trying to tell me. Why should I spend my days on the edge of the water, when I have so many miles to go? And so I have decided to hit the road myself. When I contacted Father Donovan, he sounded surprised, but he is giving me a special pensioner's dispensation for my journey.

If all goes according to plan, I'll be in Peru for the month of October. Sister Maria assures me I'm more than welcome to stay with her and her family.

I'll be right on time for the Incan festivals of Machu Picchu, Chinchero, Ollantaytaymbo and Urubamba. Even the names of these festivals are festivals, yes?

I kick off my travels in Venezuela next week. And then it's on to Guatemala for a tour of the Mayan ruins. I'm assured that Internet cafes have cropped up everywhere. So look for my postings!

And thank you, again, Irene dear, for knowing exactly what

literary lifeline to throw me. I feel reborn. I am always amazed by the power of a classic!

With affection—

Sister Soledad

I decide to save that letter in my archives, because Sister's bravery seems important to remember. Though I can hardly imagine Sister Soledad being born the first time, let alone reborn.

And all because of *On the Road*. Someday I'll reread that book.

I Break My Resolution

STARLAMALLOY'S JOURNAL

The other Day, D tried to Get Back with Me. This is 100 % True and Witnessed. But then I had an Apacalips: Nobody should Stay with Somebody who Makes you Feel like You are Not Worth It. Especially if that person Overly Relies on his Own Smartness to Make you Feel like you are Less. And also if that Same Person admitted he liked you for Surface Reasons.

What could Be Wronger than That?

From Now on, I Will not be Mentioning D in my Journals, in Words, Prose or Poems.

I Hand D to My Witness Free of Charge. Except for one Thing.

Witness—take note. I need a Discount Hair cut for school.

When I look over e-mails I've sent to Whit, I notice that sometimes my tone shifts to the style of the Heroine I am admiring at the time. But Starla always stays Starla. She knows who she is and what she wants, and she doesn't hide it. Sometimes that works even better than school smarts. I wish I could explain this to her in a way that doesn't seem condescending. Instead, I send her the link for Style to Go, which is as close as I dare to a tacit agreement on the bargain haircut.

My weeks away from Style to Go have matured me into a slightly better employee. The trick, I discover, is to repeat everything out loud. Especially when on the telephone, which is where Mom has assigned me so that I'm never actually dealing with hair.

"You said Tuesday?" I ask.

"That's right."

"Tuesday, August fifteenth?"

"That's what I said."

"Could you spell your last name again?"

"M-I-L-L-E-R."

"Okay, Ms. Miller, I am confirming a double process for Tuesday, August fifteenth–"

And then Starla walks in, and before I realize what I'm doing, I've hung up.

"Hi." It's been almost a month since I've seen her. She is wearing an oversized white button-down shirt, belted, and sandals. Not many people I know could make this outfit work. In fact, nobody.

"I need a fierce cut," she says. "My hair's too long. I

thought since you never gave me my ten dollars that day, you could shave the difference off the price."

I nod yes as the smitten Bella swirls Starla into a black robe. "You've got awesome hair," she oozes. "It's a little dry. I'm gonna give you a special deep conditioning pack, it's made with apple cider and mint, free of charge. Then Beth Ann will have a consultation with you about the cut."

"My mom," I explain.

Starla allows herself to be led to the sinks.

"You girls are friends from school?" Mom beams over at Starla as she shellacs a final coat of spray on Mrs. Irwin's curls. "I can give you a great back-to-school look when I'm finished," she calls out. "With some long layering on the sides–"

"Fierce," Starla repeats.

"Fierce, got it." Mom nods. "Choppy, but flattering angles. We'll use a razor."

"I want to start the year off brand-new," Starla says once she's been washed and seated.

I sit down in the chair next to her and swivel it so that I'm facing her like a talk-show host. "My friend Whitney is coming home tomorrow and–"

But Starla has grabbed a pair scissors out of the sanitizing jar. All at once, she chops off a hunk of hair, right in the front. "Maybe you can start from that," she tells Mom.

Everyone–Mom, me, Bella, Marianne and Mrs. Irwin–

gasps. We stare at the stump of hair that now spikes directly off Starla's forehead.

Marianne breaks the horrified silence with a laugh. "Well, now, Beth Ann. That's a challenge."

"My goodness!" On her way out the door, Mrs. Irwin scowls disapprovingly at Starla. "I hope you're pleased with yourself."

Starla does look pleased.

Mom lets the rest of us watch as she cuts Starla's hair into a style that would never go into my old notebook. Nobody speaks. We watch the black ends fall into a magic circle around the chair. When Bella comes by with the broom, a few strands blow up and stick to my ankles and underneath my flip-flops.

How weird would I be if I saved some of Starla's hair?

I put the thought out of my mind. Starla just won't stop inspiring my inner creepster.

It takes twice the time of a regular haircut, and when Mom is finished, I can see in her face that she's dissatisfied. Still, she unsnaps the robe with her usual flourish and hands Starla a mirror so that she can get a view of the back. Starla tilts this way and that.

"You like it?" asks Mom. "I was trying for French punk."

"It's crazy ugly, right?" Starla asks.

Only it's not crazy or ugly. Not on Starla Malloy. Without all her hair, Starla's eyes look twice as large. Her cheekbones appear broader, her neck swans up that much longer, and there is something delicate and vulnerable in her face that I hadn't seen before.

"Well, it's fierce," Mom pronounces doubtfully. "Like you wanted. And I had to cut a lot, to match what you started. But you've got amazing bone structure. You could wear any style, really."

"Nothing would look wrong on you," adds Bella.

Starla doesn't say anything. For a moment, she seems heartbroken. Then she jumps out of the chair and reaches for her bag, snapping open her wallet as I run to the register to take care of her bill.

"Maybe I'll see you in school?" Without asking Mom, I cut the ten dollars off the price.

"Sure," she answers, though we both doubt it. Summertime is different than school time. In summer, days melt, rules bend, and grades merge until it's September again, when time refreezes back into its own set of countdowns, its chunks of classes and cliques and schedules. It won't be long before I'm in the school cafeteria with Britta and Whitney, listening to Whit explain the calorie count on our cheese fries, while Starla sits at her scary-cool table with friends I'd be too shy to talk to.

But watching Starla go, I feel wrenched, and for a moment, I imagine us as school friends, laughing in the hallway, signaling secret jokes while other kids wonder jealously how

I, a lowly freshman without a swimming pool or driver's permit or anything special, could claim any part of Starla Malloy's attention.

Starla and I could never be friends. But watching her go, I feel wrenched.

"Bye," I say.

"Bye, Irene," she mutters under her breath as she pushes out into the heat. I'd never heard Starla say my name before.

"What a beautiful girl," says Mom.

"Beauty is not a need," I say, "but an ecstasy." My quote leaves nobody impressed. "Keats," I add, entirely for my own benefit.

"What do you think she is?" asks Bella. "Italian, Spanish, Egyptian—what?"

"Lord knows. Little bit of all of it. You can't even look too long at a girl that gorgeous," adds Marianne as she settles back in her booth. "It's like staring into an eclipse."

Mom lets out one of her classic snorts.

Starla crosses the street, her head down, her fingertips rubbing the stubble at her forehead. Her shoulders slouch, dejected, and it strikes me that the "ecstasy" part of Starla's beauty is reaped exclusively by the people who get to stare at her and make judgments.

"Girls that pretty are the luckiest girls in the world," declares Bella. "Imagine how it'd be if you had everyone looking at you and admiring you every single minute of the day?"

"The easy life," says Marianne.

"Problem free," Mom agrees.

They all stare out the storefront window, slightly peeved, as if Starla has sneaked something past them. Only I know different. "Believe me, she has exactly the same problems," I say as I watch her turn the corner and disappear.

I Become an Almost Heroine

WHEN LAINIE GETS back from Florida, I call over to the Priors and ask Judith if I can come visit for the day.

"I'm sure she'd love it," says Judith. "You know, Irene, for the life of me sometimes I couldn't figure out why, but that girl just adores you."

"Judith, I'm really sorry about her arm, and for having those kids over and everything."

She sighs. "We all make mistakes. But I have to say, there were times that you were irresponsible."

"I know."

"It wasn't lost on me that you let the kids eat ice cream for breakfast."

"I'm sorry."

"And you could be really hard on them."

"I was. I know. I'm sorry. But I was helping them build character. And character is destiny."

"Mmm." Judith pauses. Then she says, "Lainie will be happy to see you. She loves you, Irene. She copies everything you do."

But this I also know.

When the purple Hybrid pulls up, I'm waiting with a plastic jar of rainbow-bright Superblo gumballs that Drew gave me on a discount from Shady Shack. I ready myself for Judith's mini-sermon about how sugar will rot out Lainie's teeth, and am all prepared to give my weak rebuttal that Lainie really, really loves Superblos. But Judith doesn't comment on it.

Upstairs in his room, Evan is trying to build a shortwave radio. When I peek in Lainie's room, I see that she's still asleep in bed. The morning sun gilds the room, and I think how delighted Lainie would be with the princess-y way she looks right now, all the gold light on her face and her hair shining on the pillow and no cast or drool in sight. I decide I'll do a quick sketch of her. Something for her to wake up and see.

I seat myself in her chair by the window and rummage in Lainie's book bag for her markers and sketch paper, and that's when my fingers graze it. I know even before I've pulled it out that I've finally discovered my long-lost blue spiral Heroine Heads notebook.

At first, my heart pounds in horror when I see what Lainie has done to my work. On one page, she's attempted to make some heads from her own favorite books. Beezus is next to Judy Moody is next to Amber Brown, and Lainie has shamelessly copied everything: my handwriting, the way I label my heroines, the size and spacing of the heads. But I hardly have time for this specific fury, because by the next page Lainie is using the notebook as a general sketch album of portraits of everyone she has ever met in her entire life. I skim past drawings of Judith, Dan, Grandma, Gretchen McCoy, somebody named Caitlyn, somebody else named Mr. Kohler, Annie Waldron, Evan, Zaps—even Poundcake has been majestically commemorated in my book.

Then I flip to the next page and find me. My giant self, alone, takes up all the room. I am huge, with all ten of my fingers and fork-prong eyelashes and a smile like a banana wedged under my nose. Of course it doesn't look anything like me because Lainie has so little talent for capturing a likeness, but unlike any of Lainie's other drawings, my name is written in glittery pen across the top of the page, and my head and my name are both captured inside some kind of wobbly balloon. Or is it a heart?

I squint at it, turning it sideways and upside down. Balloon. No, heart. No, I can't tell.

Lainie has made me the star of my own notebook.

Except that it's her notebook now, and I'm not even that angry, maybe because this morning I feel so much older than my notebook, as if somewhere along the summer one of my time countdowns got compressed and sped me through a tunnel when I wasn't looking.

Heroine Hairstyles, what an idea. But I know I can dream another dream, and I'm not going to let myself get too embarrassed about the old one. Maybe, instead of a beauty parlor, I could open a crafts store, or a bookshop, where I'd still paint the floorboards white and serve peppermint tea—and hire someone else to do the accounting. And I still see my future intertwined with lively outdoor dinner parties overlooking the Los Angeles skyline. Some dreams should stay fixed on the horizon.

Meantime, Lainie and I can work on a few portraits together, and maybe some paper dolls, after she wakes up.